D1112782

Haunted!

"No matter what anyone says, there are no such things as ghosts, and there never were," Rob said to Jenna.

"Don't be too sure," said Dave, one of the members of the Shadow Club. "A couple of years ago—"

His words were cut off as a tall figure dressed in black came onto the path, a pickax in one gloved hand. Jenna felt herself freeze with terror. The figure used both arms to raise the pickax slowly.

Jenna gasped. She couldn't believe what she was seeing. The figure had no head!

Weekly Reader Book Club Presents

Phantom Valley

The Headless Ghost

Lynn Beach

A MINSTREL® BOOK

PUBLISHED BY POCKET BOOKS

New York London Toronto Sydney Tokyo Singapore

This book is a presentation of Newfield Publications, Inc. Newfield Publications offers book clubs for children from preschool through high school. For further information write to: **Newfield Publications, Inc.,** 4343 Equity Drive, Columbus, Ohio 43228.

Published by arrangement with Pocket Books, a division of Simon & Schuster Inc. Newfield Publications is a federally registered trademark of Newfield Publications, Inc. Weekly Reader is a federally registered trademark of Weekly Reader Corporation.

A MINSTREL PAPERBACK *ORIGINAL*

A Minstrel Book published by
POCKET BOOKS, a division of Simon & Schuster Inc.
1230 Avenue of the Americas, New York, NY 10020

ISBN 0-671-75926-4

First Minstrel Books printing December 1992

A MINSTREL BOOK and colophon are registered trademarks of Simon & Schuster Inc.

Phantom Valley is a trademark of Parachute Press, Inc.

Printed in the U.S.A.

The
Headless
Ghost

Prologue

Twenty Years Earlier

The boy was running, running through the snowy woods. Pine branches slapped at his face, but he didn't feel them. All he thought about was running. He was running faster than he had ever run before. Running to get away. Running for his life.

He thought someone was behind him. He could hear footsteps, moving closer and closer.

The boy picked up speed. Soon, he was at the edge of a ravine. He started to climb down. It was then he felt someone, or something, grab his shoulder. Terrified, he raised his head.

"No!" the boy cried. "No!" The last words he ever said were lost in the winter wind. "Jeb," he gasped. "Jeb Bendigo."

Chapter 1

"Rob, it's almost six o'clock," Jenna Black said impatiently. "We should be halfway to the Shadow Club lodge by now."

Her tall, thin stepbrother ignored her and continued to bounce his basketball on the Chilleen Academy gravel and dirt driveway. "Stop bothering me," he muttered.

"Jeff started out ten minutes ago," Jenna went on. "You know we can't be late for our final test for the Shadow Club. If we are, we've blown it."

Rob finally glanced at her, almost as if he'd just realized she was standing there. "Big deal!" he said sarcastically. "The Shadow Club is just a bunch of snobs. Why is making the club so important?"

Because everyone at Chilleen Academy thinks I'm a goody-goody, Jenna answered silently. *Because maybe if*

I join the Shadow Club, I'll be as popular as Marissa and Wendy and Del.

Out loud she said, "They're not snobs. They really do good things, like helping out at the senior citizens' center and working with recycling. *And* the kids in the Shadow Club are the most popular kids in the school."

Rob yawned. Being popular at Chilleen was not something that interested him. He only cared about his friends back home in Los Angeles. Jenna and Rob had known each other for only three years, ever since her mother married his father. From what Jenna knew, Rob had probably been born cool. Back home in Los Angeles, he had dozens of friends. At Chilleen, Jenna knew plenty of kids who wanted to hang out with him, but Rob didn't act interested.

"Only a few kids get into the club each year," she tried again. "Being chosen is a real honor."

"Oh, big honor," Rob said. "I'd trade a hundred memberships in the Shadow Club for five minutes back in L.A. with my friends."

Jenna started to answer, then shut her mouth. Rob had been sent to Chilleen after getting into a fight with the principal at his old school in Los Angeles. Jenna knew he missed his friends and didn't like Chilleen.

She found it hard to understand what there was to hate at Chilleen, though. She was in her second year, and loved it. The rustic wooden buildings and thick southwestern pine forest were home to Jenna.

Somehow she felt it was up to her to help Rob fit in.

That was why she'd talked him into trying out for the Shadow Club.

Rob shook back his dark blond hair. "This whole club thing is lame," he said. "No one bothers with this club stuff in L.A."

"The Shadow Club is really important to me," Jenna said. "Please don't mess up."

Rob tossed the basketball into a bush and shrugged. "Shadow Club, here we come."

It was getting dark as they stepped into the woods. Pine branches moved in the wind, throwing eerie shadows across the trail. The woods Jenna loved so much now seemed really spooky. She knew the original Shadow Club was started in the 1930s by a group of students who were interested in the strange things that happened in Phantom Valley.

She shivered and walked faster, eager to get to the meeting. They turned onto the path that led to the club's lodge. The lodge, a long wooden hunting cabin that had been built in the 1800s, was nearly a mile from school. It was still on Chilleen property, though. Three years earlier when the club had started up again, Mrs. Danita, the headmistress, allowed the Shadow Club members to clean up the old lodge and use it for their headquarters.

"Do you know what tests we have to pass tonight?" Jenna asked nervously, playing with a piece of her long dark brown hair.

"We have to pass something called a 'test of courage,' " Rob said in a bored voice.

5

"A test of courage!" exclaimed Jenna. "But I thought scary tests weren't allowed at Chilleen. I heard that a long time ago a boy died doing a test of courage. Do you think that's true?"

"Yeah," said Rob. "It happened about twenty years ago. The Shadow Club was shut down right after that. I wonder what the kid did and how he died."

Jenna couldn't imagine, but she thought the whole thing sounded horrible. She hoped nothing bad would happen that night. For the next few minutes she walked in silence behind Rob through the dark woods.

"How many of us do you think will make the club?" Jenna suddenly asked. "I've heard that sometimes no one gets in."

When Rob didn't answer, Jenna continued. "I bet your roommate Jeff Dearborn gets in—Mr. Perfect Grades." Rob's roommate was always trying to prove that he was better than everyone else at everything, Jenna thought. "Jeff probably got to the lodge an hour ahead of time," she said.

"BOO!" A tall figure suddenly jumped out of the trees onto the path a foot in front of them. Jenna gave a small squeal.

"You jerk," said Rob, recognizing Jeff.

"Had you going, huh?" said Jeff.

Jenna waited for her heart to slow down to normal. "We thought you'd be at the lodge by now."

Jeff gave her a grin. "It's more fun to listen in on you. I always knew you were jealous of my grades."

"Very funny." Jenna looked at Jeff. "Are you nervous about whatever it is we have to do tonight?"

"I'm never nervous about any kind of test," Jeff said. He poked Rob in the arm. "It's Rob who's nervous."

"Nothing at this stupid school makes me nervous," Rob said. "In fact, nothing here even interests me."

"Then why'd you decide to try out for the Shadow Club?" Jeff asked.

Rob gave a shrug. "I was bored, and it's something to do."

Jeff pointed up ahead to a pale, thin figure standing on the side of the path. "Hey, who's that?"

Jenna recognized Deidre Carmody, another student trying out for the Shadow Club. "I heard you guys coming and figured I'd better wait," Deidre said as they caught up to her. "That way if we're late, we'll all be late together."

Jenna noticed that Deidre didn't appear to be at all nervous. Jeff must have noticed, too, because he said, "How come you don't look worried? Getting into the Shadow Club is supposed to be scary."

"My father and four uncles were all members. It's like a family tradition," Deidre explained, pushing her black curly hair behind her ear. "I figure if they got in, I can get in."

Jeff nodded. "The way I figure it, we've all made it this far for specific reasons. Deidre, you're still in because of your family. Jenna and I are in because of our grades. They like Danny Overton because he's the total jock, and Cissy Davis because she acts just like Marissa and Wendy. But I have no idea why they want Rob."

Rob took a swipe at Jeff, and Jeff ducked. Jenna ignored their clowning, wondering what would happen next. Even if the others weren't afraid, she was getting more and more nervous by the minute.

"What's the matter, Jen?" Jeff teased. "Afraid of ghosts?"

"I just heard it can be scary," said Jenna, thinking about the kid who had died.

"Oh, come on," Rob said. "They can try to scare you, but I don't think it can be anything really bad."

"Don't be too sure of that," said Deidre. Jenna glanced at Deidre to see if she was joking, but her expression appeared to be as serious as her voice. "Getting into the Shadow Club can be really scary." Deidre went on. "Especially if you meet the ghost!"

"Welcome to the Shadow Club," Marissa Lambert said, holding a flickering candle with both hands. Marissa, the president of the club, was dressed all in black. The candlelight cast deep shadows on her face.

Jenna took a quick look around the darkened lodge. Several candles lit the wood-paneled room. At the far end of the lodge a fire was burning in the big stone fireplace. Pushed back against the walls was lots of rough pine furniture. The six kids who were trying out for the club were sitting in a circle on the floor in the center of the cabin.

At one end of the room about twelve club members stood in a line behind Marissa. Jenna recognized only Wendy Baron, Tamara, Dave, and James. They were all cool, a little wild, and very popular. *Did they have to act that way to be in the club?* Jenna wondered. *Or were they like that before they joined?*

"You six are the only ones who have survived the first tests for membership. The final tests will be much tougher," Marissa went on. "Tonight, we test your courage. We'll ask you to do things—dangerous things—to prove you really want to be a member of the Shadow Club. If you want out, now's the time to speak up."

No one moved. Marissa nodded and said, "Whether or not you get into the Shadow Club, you must keep its secrets. Tonight's events must stay completely secret. You must swear never to tell anyone what you see or hear."

"What if we tell?" asked Rob. "I mean, if I don't get in, why should I keep your secrets?"

Jenna stared at her stepbrother in disbelief. It figured Rob would give Marissa a hard time.

"You're breaking school rules just by being here," Wendy Baron, the vice-president, said. "Secret ceremonies aren't allowed at Chilleen. But tonight, our advisor Mr. Tam and most of the other teachers are away on a retreat. They'll never know what goes on here—unless one of you talks. If anyone tells, we're *all* in serious trouble." She smiled at Rob. "Do you really want to get thrown out of another school?"

Rob smiled back at her and said, "Believe me, I wish I could leave."

"Any other questions?" asked Marissa. When there were none, she said, "Then raise your right hands and repeat after me."

The six kids in the center all raised their hands and repeated together: "I swear never to tell anyone the secrets of the Shadow Club. What I see and do tonight will stay a secret even if I do not get into the club."

"Good," said Marissa. "Now we'll seal the oath." She lifted a glass pitcher from a small wooden table at the side of the room. The pitcher held a thick, dark red liquid. "You will each come up to the table and take a glass," she said. "Then you'll seal your oaths by drinking the sacred blood."

"The *what?*" shrieked Cissy.

"Haven't you ever heard of a blood oath?" Marissa asked. She started to pour the thick red liquid into each of the glasses. "The blood makes sure you'll never tell."

"What kind of blood is it?" Rob asked suspiciously.

Marissa handed a glass to Deidre. "Cow's blood. From one of the ranches in Phantom Valley. Why are you all waiting? Come on, unless you're wimping out."

Jenna couldn't believe she was doing as she was told. Like the other five kids, though, she took a glass. *It's not really cow's blood*, she told herself. *It's just a trick.* Still, it looked exactly like blood. She dipped a finger in it. It was thick like blood.

Holding her breath, Jenna forced herself to drink the

thick fluid. She drank it as fast as she could, but she couldn't miss the salty taste. It *was* blood, and she had just swallowed it!

Then Jenna recognized the aftertaste. It was sweet, like fruit juice. She smiled as she realized that it had been a trick. They had only added stuff to fruit juice.

Jenna saw Deidre raise her glass and choke down the liquid. "Yuck!" she gasped.

Jenna glanced at Rob. His glass was empty and he was still acting bored. Beside him, Jeff was positively green. Jenna wished she could tell them it wasn't really blood.

Just then there was a loud thump, as if a huge rock had landed on the roof of the cabin. "What's that?" Marissa asked, raising her eyes to the ceiling, her expression puzzled.

THUMP! That time the sound was even louder. A moment later there was a frightened scream from outside the cabin. Without warning a breeze swept through the room, causing all the candle flames to flicker. Jenna held her breath, her heart racing.

"What *is* that?" Marissa cried, staring at the back wall of the lodge.

The six pledges turned, their eyes following Marissa's gaze. There, floating just above the floor of the cabin, was a faintly glowing round object. While Jenna watched, her heart in her throat, the thing turned to reveal a face of something that had once been human.

"What is that?" Cissy whispered, sounding terrified. "Is that someone's head?"

"It's nothing," Jenna said, trying to sound calmer than she felt. She remembered what Rob had said about how none of the scary stuff could be really bad. "It's just a joke. Just a joke to scare us." She looked at Marissa, sure she'd be smiling. The club president's face was frozen in horror.

Then the head began to move toward the center of the room. Marissa screamed again. "No!" she cried. "No! Go away! This isn't supposed to happen!"

The features on the face were twisted in horror. Greenish flesh hung from below the deep-set eyes. Jenna felt herself shake as its black lips curled up in a creepy smile, and it began to laugh.

Chapter 2

The head moved closer and Jenna became more terrified. Danny ran for the door, and she took off with
him. Glancing back over her shoulder, she saw the
floating head still there. Its mouth continued to grin
crazily.

"Let me out!" Danny shouted, tugging on the door.
"Let me out of here!"

Jenna was right behind him, and the other kids were
behind her. The door was locked.

"Try the window!" cried Jeff. Jenna turned, but at
that moment Wendy's voice cut through the noise.
"Stop!" she shouted. "Stop! It's okay. It's gone.
Look!"

Her heart still hammering, Jenna saw that the glowing head had disappeared.

"Not bad," said Rob, sounding as if he hadn't been

scared. "I guess you must have hung the head from a string on the ceiling, but how'd you get it to glow?"

"That wasn't a trick," said Tamara. She was a tall chestnut-haired girl, secretary of the Shadow Club and chief photographer for the school yearbook. At the moment she was very pale.

"You'd better sit down," said Wendy, sounding shaken. "We've just had a visit from Jeb Bendigo, and it's time you knew his story and why he showed up tonight."

Marissa stood in front of the fireplace and waited while they all sat down. "Jeb Bendigo was a miner in Phantom Valley a little more than a hundred years ago," she began. "He lived in a cabin about a quarter of a mile from here and struck gold exactly one year after he came to Phantom Valley. There were some people in the valley who were jealous of Jeb. He was riding into town to file his claim when he ran into a wire someone had strung across the trail."

"What do you mean, a wire?" Danny asked.

Marissa drew an imaginary line across her throat. "It was stretched across the trail this high. He galloped straight into it."

Jenna thought of the floating head, and a sick feeling went through her. "You mean the wire cut off Jeb Bendigo's head?"

"Gross!" cried Deidre.

"It's true," said Wendy. "And there's more."

Marissa went on with the story. "After Bendigo died,

the other miners went to check out his claim. They didn't find any gold. All they found was a pile of fool's gold."

"What's that?" asked Cissy.

"Pyrite," answered Jeff. "It's a metal that looks like gold but isn't worth much. A lot of people mistake it for the real thing."

"Exactly," said Wendy. "Old Jeb didn't know that his 'gold' was just pyrite. Even now, long after his death, he guards his treasure. He continues to haunt these woods and protect his cabin.

"From the time the Shadow Club was started until it was shut down," Wendy went on, "there was a very special tradition. Each year two kids who wanted to be members of the club were chosen to visit Bendigo's cabin. They had to go there late at night and come back with a piece of fool's gold. Sometimes strange things happened to the kids who were chosen."

"What kind of things?" asked Rob, curious.

"One boy's hair turned white overnight. A girl lost her voice for six months. They said it was because of fright," Marissa answered. "Finally, twenty years ago, one of the kids who went into Jeb's cabin was killed."

"He died?" asked Danny in disbelief. "In the cabin?"

"No," Wendy explained. "They say Jeb chased the kid through the woods and scared him to death. The boy was found in a ravine right in the Phantom Valley woods—with his neck broken."

"That doesn't prove he was killed by a ghost. He probably lost his way and fell," Rob said, challenging her.

"Maybe," Marissa said. "No one can be sure. But we do know one thing . . . the student who was killed was the *last one* to go into Jeb's cabin . . . until now. Tonight, two of you will be chosen to go into the cabin."

Rob started laughing. "This is supposed to scare us, right?"

Jenna couldn't believe her stepbrother found all this funny. Just the thought of going into a haunted cabin made her shiver. As Marissa continued to speak, Jenna watched the flames in the fireplace dance. "In just a moment we'll choose the two people to visit Jeb Bendigo's cabin."

Marissa, Wendy, and the rest of the members went to the far side of the room, leaving Jenna and the others thinking about the ghost.

Rob glanced around. "All right, if you're all so spooked, I'll go to the cabin."

"You looked scared to me when Jeb Bendigo's head was floating around this room," Jeff pointed out.

"I can't believe you guys. That wasn't Jeb Bendigo's head," Rob said. "That was a trick."

"Probably," said Jenna, wanting to believe he was right. "Besides, there are no such things as ghosts, right?"

"So, do *you* want to go to the cabin?" asked Jeff.

Before Jenna could answer, Wendy walked over, carrying a lit black candle. Beside her, Marissa held a black cup. Inside the cup were six thin straws.

"These are the straws of choice," Marissa said. She reached into the cup, pulled the straws out, and showed them to everyone. One end of each straw had been painted. Two were red, two were yellow, and two were blue.

"Those who pick the blue straws," Marissa went on, "must visit the Chilleen graveyard by moonlight and come back with a cupful of soil dug from the grave of Morgana Chilleen. Those choosing the yellow ones will go to Shadow Village and bring back some proof that you were there."

Marissa continued with her speech. "And the two who draw red straws—will go to Jeb Bendigo's cabin."

Jenna felt a shiver run through her. She didn't believe in ghosts, but she really hoped she wouldn't have to go into Jeb's cabin.

Marissa put the straws back into the cup, with the colored tips down. Then she shook the cup around so no one could tell which straw was which. She held out the cup.

Jeff picked first. He got a yellow-tipped straw. Jenna couldn't believe that he was actually upset about it. Danny and Cissy were next. Their straws were both blue. Rob picked the second yellow straw.

"Looks like I win the grand prize," Deidre said when the cup came to her. She reached out for a red-tipped straw.

Jenna took her straw, knowing that it, too, had to be red. She studied it a moment, her heart beating fast. *It's only a test,* she told herself. *Ghosts aren't real.*

"Congratulations," said Marissa. "You two get to bring tradition back to the Shadow Club. Tomorrow night we'll give you a map. In the light of the moon, you must go through the woods to Jeb Bendigo's cabin. Each of you will go inside and bring back one piece of fool's gold as proof that you were there. Then you'll come back to the lodge—if you can."

"What if the gold isn't there anymore?" Deidre asked.

"Then you'll have to bring some other proof that you went into the cabin," Tamara answered.

"This isn't fair," Jeff said suddenly. "Shadow Village is easy. Why can't I go to Bendigo's cabin, too?"

"Because you chose the yellow straw," said Marissa coldly. "Each of the tests is important, so stop complaining."

"This whole thing is dumb," Rob muttered under his breath.

"You wouldn't think so if you were going to Bendigo's cabin," said James.

"I'd think it was stupid if I were going to the moon," said Rob. "This whole thing about the spirits in Phantom Valley is just garbage. I can't believe any of you really believes it."

"Maybe you'll feel differently after tomorrow night," Marissa said. "You'll get your maps tomorrow evening after dinner. You must find a way to leave the Academy without being seen. When you've finished your tests, meet back at the lodge for judgment. Remember, we've got to get back to the school before lights-out, so you don't have a lot of time."

Marissa, Wendy, and the other members of the club blew out the candles. The first part of the courage test was over. Everyone left the lodge together and set off for school.

Marissa suddenly stopped on the path as if she were waiting for something. "Come on," called Tamara. "Let's go."

"Wait a minute," said Marissa. She fell to her knees on the path and began brushing aside dirt and leaves. A long, narrow strip of wood was exposed. "That's funny," she said in a puzzled voice.

"What?" said Deidre.

"Where's Del?" Marissa said. "Del?" she called. And then, a moment later, louder: "Del!"

"What's going on?" Jeff whispered. "Why is she yelling at the ground?"

"Probably another trick," said Rob, bored.

"Del?" Marissa called again. "Del, are you all right?" She sounded frightened now, and the other members of the club quickly gathered around her.

"There's a coffin buried here," Wendy quickly explained. "Del was supposed to jump out of it and scare you. But something must have gone wrong. James, how long ago did you bury him?"

"About half an hour ago," James said. "He said it was cool. There shouldn't be any problem."

Marissa and the others continued to uncover the lid of the coffin. "Help me!" she called. "There's no time to lose!"

Two other members of the club knelt down and began helping her. After a moment they could see the top of the polished black coffin.

"Del! Del!" Marissa called his name again and again. She sounded panicked, almost in tears.

"We've got it now," said Dave. "Come on, someone help me with the lid."

Quickly Dave, James, and Marissa pulled open the heavy coffin lid. Marissa leaned over and put her hand in the coffin. Her face became pale and she shook her head. "No!" she screamed, the one word filled with disbelief. "This couldn't have happened."

"What is it?" Wendy cried.

Marissa acted as if she didn't hear her. "It was supposed to be a joke," she said. "He was going to jump out of the coffin to scare you!"

"Marissa!" Wendy shook her.

Marissa raised her head with tears in her eyes. "He's dead," she said slowly. "Del Robins is dead."

Chapter 3

"**H**e's dead," Marissa said again.

"No!" cried Wendy. "It can't be!" She bent over the grave and peered into the coffin. "Del," she whispered.

Marissa's voice shook. "He must have run out of air."

Jenna realized it was true. Somehow their trick had gone horribly wrong.

"Wait a minute," said Rob, sounding suspicious. "Let me see that coffin . . ." He pushed through the crowd to lean over the open grave.

Suddenly a hand covered with rotting green flesh shot out of the coffin. Jenna shrieked as she saw the arm stretch toward her stepbrother's throat.

"No! No!" Jenna screamed and tried to pull Rob away. Jenna screamed again as the hideous green corpse slowly sat up. And then the body reached up and peeled off its head.

21

"Booga, booga!" the corpse shouted in Del's voice and grinned. "It is *so* boring to lie around in a coffin all evening."

Marissa clapped her hands together. "Good work, Del."

Jenna's heart was beating wildly, and her knees felt weak. She couldn't believe it was Del who had scared her so much.

"I told you it was a trick," Rob muttered, even though he still seemed shaken up.

"Pretty good, don't you think?" said Wendy, smiling widely.

"I—I really thought he was dead!" said Jenna, angry that they had frightened her so much.

"I bet Bendigo's head was another trick," Rob said. "And so was that 'blood.' I know it was fruit juice."

Tamara smiled. "That's for us to know and you to find out."

"We'd better get back to school before lights-out," said Marissa. "Del, close up the coffin. Come on, guys."

The walk back to the school was quiet. "Get a good night's sleep, everyone," Marissa said as Chilleen Academy came into sight. "You'll want to be rested up for tomorrow night's tests of courage. We want all of you to have a fair chance to make the club."

Do you really? Jenna wondered. She wished she knew how the members of the Shadow Club really felt about her. She thought about Marissa and Wendy, Tamara,

James, Dave, and Del. They always seemed to be in the center of whatever was going on at Chilleen. The meeting that night had been scary, but she still wanted to be part of the club. It was worth going into a haunted cabin.

Her thoughts were interrupted by a sudden loud howl. "What was that?" cried Deidre. It was the first time Deidre had sounded frightened, and Jenna wondered what sort of partner she would make for the test of courage. Deidre was in her biology class, but they didn't know each other all that well.

"That's just a coyote," said Del. "It's nothing. There are lots of worse things in the Phantom Valley woods."

Yeah, Jenna thought. *Like a cabin haunted by a headless ghost!*

Chapter 4

"**J**enna, can you tell the class the main cause of the War of 1812?"

Jenna looked up and blinked.

Mrs. Douglas, her history teacher, frowned at her. "Next time," she said, "pay attention."

"Sorry." Jenna felt herself blushing. Usually paying attention wasn't a problem. That day, though, all she could think about was the upcoming test of courage. *It's no big deal*, she told herself for the tenth time. *All I have to do is walk through the woods and go into an old cabin. And then, afterward, I'll be a member of the Shadow Club—I hope.*

The other kids in class don't know what I'm going to do tonight, she realized. The only ones who knew were the ones trying out for and the actual members of the club. Wendy Baron was in her class, and she gave Jenna a secret smile. It already felt as if she were part of a special group.

She was supposed to meet the others after supper at the edge of the woods to get her map. The day crawled by for Jenna. Every class dragged.

Finally it was dinner time, and she was standing in the dining hall with her tray, looking for a place to sit. Rob walked by her.

"Hey, wait up," Jenna called out. Rob kept on walking, though. Jenna ran after him to a table by the window.

"So," Rob said, making a face at his plate of meat-loaf. "Ready for the big night?"

"I go between being scared and being excited," Jenna confessed. "What about you?"

"Actually, I'd *like* to see a ghost. It'd be the first interesting thing that's happened to me here."

"Rob," Jenna said, "they may not let you into the club if you don't watch what you say."

Rob shrugged. "Stop telling me what to do, Jenna. Besides, who cares? I'm just doing this until I find a way to get myself back home to California. All this club stuff is stupid."

He turned to her and continued. "What I don't get, though, is why *you* want to be a part of that club. Those kids don't seem like your kind of kids at all—they're a little too wild for you."

Jenna was annoyed. "You're not the only one who can be daring. I like the kids in the Shadow Club. And I think they like me!"

25

"You know," Rob said slowly, "I don't think it's an accident that you're going to Bendigo's cabin tonight."

"What do you mean?" Jenna asked. "I picked a red straw."

"I think Marissa knew you were scared and fixed it so you'd get the scariest test."

"How?" Jenna demanded.

Rob shrugged again. "I don't know, but they managed to make a head float. I think they could find a way to set you up for tonight."

It was a breezy early-November night. The weather had been unusually warm that fall. The moon had just begun to rise, and the forest path was clear ahead. Jenna and Deidre were off school property and past the lodge. They knew it was a quarter mile to Bendigo's cabin, but in the dark and following a bobbing flashlight it was hard to tell how far they'd gone. Jenna had never gone this far into the woods. There wasn't a single thing she recognized. Everywhere she turned, the trees seemed to go on forever.

She stopped where the trail split into two. "Which way?" she asked.

Deidre checked the hand-drawn map she held. "This says we go to the right."

"Good," Jenna said. "It's wider that way." As the girls moved on, though, the path suddenly became narrow and covered over with weeds.

"What do we do now?" Deidre asked.

Jenna shone the flashlight on the map and frowned. From what she could tell the path they were on should have kept going straight and then curved around some low hills to the old miner's cabin. "We must have done something wrong," Jenna decided. "We probably should have taken the other path. Let's go back."

"I don't believe this," said Deidre. "What if we're really lost?"

Jenna wondered the same thing. "Maybe we just read the map wrong," she said calmly, but couldn't stop the shiver from running up her spine.

They started back down the path. The moon moved behind a cloud, and for the first time Jenna was aware of all the noises in the forest night. Somewhere nearby an owl hooted. Then there was another sound—one she couldn't place. "What's that?" she asked.

"What's what?" said Deidre.

"That sound." She paused to listen, then whispered, "In the bushes at the side of the path. It sounds like branches breaking. As if someone—or some*thing*—is walking beside us."

"No one's walking beside us," Deidre said calmly.

"I read there are mountain lions around here," Jenna went on. "And bears."

"Not in the valley," said Deidre. "In the mountains."

How can Deidre be so calm? Jenna wondered. *Maybe I got the hardest test*, she thought, *but at least I've got a partner who doesn't scare easily.*

27

At last they reached the fork in the path and started up the other trail.

"Everything's going to be okay," Deidre said. "I'm sure this is the right way to go." After a moment she stopped to study the map again. "I think Bendigo's cabin is just past that hill."

Around the next bend in the path they saw a large shadowy form. As the girls got closer they could see it was the ruins of an old cabin. It was smaller than the lodge and in much worse shape. The windows were boarded up, and the front steps looked as if someone had taken an ax to them. The roof was sagging into the building and the wood gave off a moldy, wet smell.

"This can't be it," Jenna said with a shudder.

"It has to be," said Deidre, pointing to the map.

"But this—this place looks like no one's been here in more than a hundred years."

The girls stopped and shone their flashlights on the spooky old cabin. It wasn't hard to imagine the headless ghost of the old miner, waiting there, guarding a treasure that was never a treasure at all.

A groaning sound suddenly came from inside the cabin.

"Did you hear that?" Jenna whispered.

"It's probably just the rotten wood sagging," Deidre answered.

She was starting to sound less cool, though, Jenna noticed. The hair on the back of her neck prickled. "Come on," Jenna said, taking a deep breath. "Let's go in and get the fool's gold." She took a step toward the front door of the cabin and stopped.

"It's okay," Deidre said. "I'll go first."

Jenna shrugged and stepped aside. Deidre shone her flashlight in front of her and made her way up the broken steps to the doorway.

Jenna was about to follow her inside when she heard Deidre scream.

Chapter 5

"**D**eidre!" Jenna cried.

Deidre stood frozen just inside the doorframe, her scream still ringing in the forest. Finally she ran out and started down the path again.

Jenna took off after her. "Deidre, wait! What happened?"

Deidre finally slowed down. She stood bent over, breathing hard, her hands on her knees.

"Are you okay?" Jenna asked.

Deidre's voice shook. "I'm not going back in there."

"That's all right," Jenna said, trying to calm her. "Just tell me what scared you."

Deidre stood up. "Bats."

Jenna stared at the other girl. Deidre's face was white in the flashlight's beam, white as if she'd really seen a ghost. "You got scared by a *bat?*"

"A bunch of bats," Deidre said. "A whole lot of them. They're hanging from the rafters just inside the doorway. I'll bet anything there are lots more inside the cabin."

"They must live in there," said Jenna.

Deidre shuddered. "I've heard there are at least a hundred bats in some kinds of bat colonies. I'm not going into any broken-down cabin with a hundred bats in it!"

Jenna couldn't believe how Deidre had changed. Earlier she had acted as if she didn't care if she met a ghost. Yet, seeing bats had totally terrified her.

"I'm sorry," Deidre said. "I'm more scared of bats than anything on earth."

"I guess I know how you feel," Jenna said. "I feel almost the same way about spiders."

"I mean, you'll have to go in there alone," Deidre said.

Jenna nodded, the blood pounding loud in her ears.

"Jenna," Deidre said, "do you think that maybe when you pick up your piece of gold, you could pick up one for me, and—"

"And then tell the others you went in?" Jenna finished. "You mean, lie to them?"

Deidre pleaded, "I don't want you to have to lie, but I really can't go in there, Jenna. I can't even get near the cabin. And I—I have to get into the club. If I don't, my father will be so upset. He was in it and so were my uncles and—"

"I don't know," Jenna said.

"Please," Deidre begged. "I promise I'll wait right here until you come out."

A cool breeze picked up and Jenna shivered. She knew she couldn't change Deidre's mind.

"All right," she said. "It can't hurt to take two pieces instead of one."

"Thanks," said Deidre, giving her a quick hug. "I'll never forget you for this."

Taking a deep breath, Jenna walked back toward the cabin where Jeb Bendigo once lived. She picked her way up the broken steps and pushed the heavy wood door open all the way.

Jenna turned on her flashlight, running its beam along the inside of the cabin. Instantly a flutter of wings and a high chittering sound filled the air. The bats were everywhere, flying at crazy angles, rushing for the door.

Jenna ducked and held back a scream. *They're just bats*, she told herself. *They won't hurt me. The important thing is finding the fool's gold.*

She waited until the bats had left, then began her search. The cabin was even more run-down inside than out. The floor and roof were rotted and full of holes, and the only furniture was a broken chair and a sagging old bed. She heard something moving by the blackened stone fireplace. A second later a small, dark form darted over the top of her sneaker.

Jenna shrieked and then took a deep breath. *It's just a field mouse*, she told herself. *Probably more scared of me than I am of it.*

She walked farther into the cabin, shining her flashlight into every corner, checking for the barest glimmer of pyrite. With her every step, the floorboards creaked. A dirty cupboard hung from the far wall. Carefully Jenna pulled it open. She covered her mouth and nose as a thick cloud of dust filled the air. Was there something glimmering on the bottom shelf? She leaned forward to check it out and felt the strings of a cobweb stick to her face and hair.

She pulled back, frantically brushing the cobwebs away. A voice in her head kept screaming: *Get out of here! Get out now while there's still time!*

First, though, she had to find the fool's gold. Again Jenna swung the flashlight through the room. This time she saw it, a dark roundish shape under the bed frame. She knelt down, reached carefully under, and began to tug at the bundle. It didn't move easily—it weighed more than she had thought.

At last she pulled it out. *It's just an old rotting burlap sack,* she realized. Then she had a terrible thought. *Please,* she prayed, *don't let it be Jeb Bendigo's head inside the sack.* She forced herself to peer inside.

Her heart slowed as she realized she was staring at a bagful of glittering golden stones. The pyrite! She'd found the treasure.

"Jeb, if you're here, please don't be angry," she said aloud. "I'm only taking one little piece and I'm doing it for a good reason."

Jenna pocketed a piece of the golden pyrite, pushed

the burlap bag back under the bed and stood up. She was almost at the door when she remembered the piece for Deidre.

Jenna ran back across the rotting floorboards. Again, she bent down and stuck her hand under the bed. Something brushed against her hand.

Great, she thought, *more cobwebs.*

She shone the flashlight under the bed, and froze. It wasn't cobwebs on her hand but a hairy spider the size of a teacup. It began to crawl up her wrist.

Jenna shrieked and jumped backward. Her arm hit the bed frame, knocking the spider off. Her whole body was shaking. The spider was on the burlap bag now. Jenna reached out and tugged on the far end. The spider inched toward her. Willing herself not to scream, she reached into the bag, grabbed a second piece of pyrite, and raced out of the cabin.

Outside, she took deep gulps of the cool night air.

"Jenna?" It was Deidre. "Are you all right?"

"I've got it," Jenna said. "I got the fool's gold."

"You got two pieces?" Deidre asked in a small voice.

Jenna smiled. "One for each of us." She pressed one of the stones into Deidre's hand.

Deidre couldn't meet her eyes. "I'm so ashamed," she said. "But I couldn't let a bat keep me out of the club."

"Remember what Marissa said, though," Jenna said. "The test of courage is only one of the tests for membership."

"I know," said Deidre. "But, well . . . I didn't tell you, but Marissa practically told me I'm in the club if I pass the test. So now, thanks to you . . . everything's going to work out."

She gave Jenna a big smile and Jenna couldn't help smiling back. "Don't worry, Deidre," she said. "This will be our secret. I promise, I'll never tell the others that you didn't go in."

By the time Jenna and Deidre got to the Shadow Club lodge, Jenna was feeling excited and happy. She touched the piece of fool's gold in her pocket as if it were a good-luck charm. *There's no way we won't make the Shadow Club,* she thought.

Lanterns and candles shone through the windows of the lodge. Maybe it was because they'd just come from Bendigo's cabin, but the Shadow Club actually looked friendly to Jenna.

"Where have you two been?" Marissa said, meeting the girls at the door of the lodge. "We were getting ready to send out a search party."

"We got a little lost," Jenna admitted.

"But we found the cabin," Deidre said. She held out her piece of fool's gold. "Here's the proof."

Marissa took the pyrite and checked it, then passed it on to Wendy. "Jenna?" she said.

Jenna handed over her piece of pyrite as well. For just a second, when it left her hand, she felt a strange shiver.

"Congratulations," said Marissa. "You've passed your test of courage."

"You and Danny are the only ones who did," added Wendy, appearing at the door. Jenna and Deidre followed the leaders of the club inside. Sitting in chairs in a circle were Rob, Jeff, Cissy, and Danny. Danny looked happy, Cissy and Jeff looked upset, and Rob just looked bored.

"What happened?" Jenna asked.

"Cissy didn't want to dig up the earth from Morgana Chilleen's grave," Wendy said. "She took some from outside the graveyard and thought we'd be fooled."

Cissy stared at the floor. "The idea of taking earth from someone's grave grossed me out."

"It was supposed to," Marissa snapped. "That was part of the test."

"What happened to Jeff and Rob?" Deidre wanted to know.

"They were supposed to find something unusual to prove they'd been to Shadow Village," said Marissa. "But what did they bring back?" She opened her hand to show two small flint arrowheads.

"They came from Shadow Village!" Jeff protested. "Come back with me and I'll show you exactly where we got them!"

"Arrowheads can be picked up anywhere around Chilleen," said Tamara.

Marissa cleared her throat. "It's getting late, and we've got to get back to school before lights-out. You'll all be told tomorrow who—if anyone—gets in the club."

"So you two actually went to Jeb Bendigo's cabin?" Jeff asked Jenna and Deidre, as they walked back along the moonlit path with Rob, Cissy, and Danny. Behind them, the members of the Shadow Club were closing up the lodge for the night.

Jenna nodded.

"I wish I'd gotten to go," said Jeff.

"I can't believe you guys brought back arrowheads," said Deidre. "Didn't you know they wanted something unusual?"

"That's easy for *you* to say," said Jeff. "Everyone knows you're going to get into the club."

"What do you mean?" said Deidre.

"You've got everything they're looking for," Jeff said. "You have good grades, and you're popular, and your father was in the club."

"My four uncles, too," said Deidre. "But that doesn't mean I'll get in." Jenna remembered what Deidre had told her, though. She knew Deidre was going to get into the club.

"I wonder how many of us will make it," said Jeff.

"Maybe all of us," said Jenna. "I hope so, anyway."

"You guys are so stupid," Rob said suddenly. Jenna looked at him with surprise. It was the first time he'd said anything since they'd left the lodge. "None of this stuff matters," he went on. "The so-called test of courage is just a joke. They know how many new members they'll accept. It's exactly two."

"What are you talking about?" said Jenna.

"While we were waiting for you two to come back from Bendigo's cabin, I went outside for a walk. I heard Marissa and Wendy talking. There's a limit to the number of total members, and this semester they can take only two. One girl and one boy."

"You must have heard wrong," said Deidre.

"You'll see tomorrow," said Rob. "And you'll see that they made you go through all this garbage for nothing."

"That can't be right," said Jeff, angry now. "You mean all this stuff—the test, and the cow's blood, and everything—"

"It's all a joke. The members of the Shadow Club don't care about any of us."

I don't believe this, Jenna thought. *If what Rob says is true, it means that Deidre will be the one girl chosen for the club.* Feeling sad, Jenna dropped back a little from the others.

"Hey, wait up," came a voice from behind her. She turned to see Marissa.

"Hi, Marissa," Jenna said, trying to sound cheerful.

"We thought you guys were going to wait for us," Marissa said. "I thought we'd all walk back together. The woods aren't exactly safe at night."

"Right," said Rob. "There are terrifying owls and rabbits, and sometimes even a skunk."

"I was thinking more of the spirits," said Marissa.

Rob laughed. "No matter what anyone says, there are no such things as ghosts, and there never were."

"Don't be too sure," said Dave, another one of the members. "A couple of years ago—"

His words were cut off as a tall figure dressed in black came onto the path, a pickax in one gloved hand. Jenna felt herself freeze with terror. The figure used both arms to raise the pickax slowly.

Jenna gasped. She couldn't believe what she was seeing. The figure had no head!

Chapter 6

The figure in black raised its pickax and came toward Jenna and the others. For a long, awful moment the woods rang with screams.

"Run!" cried Marissa.

Jenna took off, then just as suddenly stopped. She remembered how well Marissa had acted scared in the lodge and at the coffin when Del was pretending to be dead.

"Wait a minute!" Jenna called out. The headless figure darted off the path and into the woods.

"Come back here!" Rob shouted and started after it. A moment later he returned to the path, laughing. "Good trick, Marissa," he said.

"It wasn't a trick!" Marissa insisted, still looking terrified.

"Come on, Marissa," said Deidre. "This has to be another joke, right? Another test of courage."

40

"That thing wasn't a trick," said Wendy. She, too, looked frightened. She moved closer to Marissa. "Maybe we went too far," she whispered.

"What do you mean?" said Jeff. "What do you mean, you went too far?"

"We wanted to scare you guys," said Wendy. "But . . . we should never have sent anyone to Bendigo's cabin."

"Do you really think this has something to do with Jeb Bendigo?" asked Deidre.

Marissa nodded. "The headless ghost. The pickax. We just—we never thought it could really happen."

The club president stared into the woods where the ghost had disappeared and gave a little shiver. "I just think—what's that?" She bent down to the side of the path, stretched out her hand, then stood up and opened her hand. "Look," she said. Jenna crowded around with the others.

In the palm of Marissa's hand was a small piece of fool's gold.

That night Jenna couldn't sleep. She had stayed in Rob and Jeff's room for a while, talking about what had happened. Rob was sure that Marissa had faked the whole scene with the headless ghost, but Jeff thought it was real. Jenna wasn't sure. She tossed and turned all night thinking about it. She didn't believe in ghosts—but she kept remembering the shivers that ran through her when she'd given the fool's gold to Marissa.

I don't care if there is a ghost, she thought. *I just want to get into the club.*

The next morning Jenna was awakened by a rustling noise. She opened one sleepy eye and saw that an envelope had been slipped under her door. Curious, she got out of bed and picked it up, then felt her heart begin to beat excitedly. Her name was printed in the center of the envelope, and in the upper left-hand corner was written: "The Shadow Club."

She sat on the edge of her bed and turned the envelope over. *Please,* she thought. *Please let me be in the club.* Carefully, so as not to tear it, Jenna opened the envelope and pulled out a single folded sheet of paper.

She read the short message, then read it again. "Welcome," it said, "to the Shadow Club. Meeting today after classes at the lodge."

"I made it!" Jenna cried aloud, happy that she had no roommate to wake. She couldn't believe it. Rob was wrong, she thought, and she couldn't wait to tell him. After dressing, she ran to Rob and Jeff's room and knocked on their door. It was opened by a sleepy-looking Rob.

"Rob, I made the club!"

"Congratulations," he said dryly. "See, everything always works out for you."

"What about you guys?" Jenna asked.

"I guess I'll just have to manage without being a member of the Shadow Club," Rob said, not acting at all upset. He showed Jenna his letter, which read: "Thanks for trying out for the club. Better luck next time."

"What about Jeff?"

"Ask him yourself," said Rob, pointing down the hall. Jeff was walking toward them, eating a muffin from his early breakfast. One look at his face told Jenna he hadn't made the club either.

"You got in," Jeff said, when he saw Jenna's smile. "Well, I don't think it's fair. I did what they said. I went on their stupid test of courage. Can I help it if Rob thought it was cool to pick up arrowheads?"

"Oh, sure," Rob said. "Blame me."

"It's not just you," Jeff admitted. "Jenna got in, and you know why? Because she went to Bendigo's cabin. Anyone who drew the red straw for Bendigo's cabin was going to get in."

Jenna didn't know what to say. She wasn't surprised that Rob hadn't made the club. After all, he had kept telling Marissa and Wendy how dumb he thought it was. Still, she was surprised Jeff wasn't chosen. She crossed to the wing on the other side of the building and climbed the stairs to Deidre's room.

She knocked on the door. There was no answer. She was about to leave when the door opened and Deidre stood there, tear stains on her face. "Deidre, what's wrong?"

"What do you think?" said Deidre. "I didn't make the club."

"You didn't make—"

"I can't believe they made us go through all that," Deidre said bitterly. "What's my father going to say?"

Jenna couldn't hide her surprise. "I'm sorry," she said. "I was sure you'd make it."

"You must feel pretty bad, too," Deidre said.

"Well, actually, I—I made the club."

"You did?" Deidre said, shocked. "But—but we passed the same test. How could they choose you and not me?"

"I don't know," said Jenna. "Maybe Rob was right. Maybe they never meant to take more than one girl."

"And you were the one," said Deidre. For a moment she looked as if she might start crying again. Instead she took a deep breath and gave Jenna a shaky smile. "Congratulations," she said, holding out her hand. "If I couldn't make it, I'm glad you did."

"Thanks," Jenna said. "I just wish it could have been both of us."

Jenna had never felt as happy as she did when the school day was finally over and she set out for the Shadow Club. She was about to go to a meeting as a full member, as part of the group she'd been dying to join since her first day at Chilleen. It felt as if her whole life was about to change. She was about to step through the door to become a part of the coolest group of kids at Chilleen.

Mr. Tam, the advisor, opened the door for her. "Here she is, our new member," he said warmly. "Congratulations, Jenna."

"Thanks," she said, smiling. A few minutes later Danny Overton entered and was given the same greeting. Jenna grinned at Marissa and Wendy, but they didn't even look at her. They were in a corner, whispering together.

This meeting, Jenna learned, was about the annual dinner for the senior citizens of the Silverbell Retirement Home that the club gave every year. "Do I have volunteers for preparing or serving the food?" Mr. Tam asked.

No one said anything. Mr. Tam seemed a little annoyed as he said, "I have to go to another meeting in a few minutes, so let's get going. Any volunteers?"

A little nervously Jenna raised her hand. "I've done a lot of cooking for my family," she said. "I know a recipe for a great vegetable soup. I could make that for the first course."

"Good," said Mr. Tam, writing her name on a piece of paper. "Are there other volunteers? What about setting up the tables and doing the shopping?"

To Jenna's surprise, no one else volunteered. "I guess I could be in charge of table setting, too," she added.

"Good idea," Wendy said with a laugh. "In fact, why don't we let Jenna do the whole dinner?"

"Very funny," said Mr. Tam. "If we don't get more volunteers, we can't have the dinner."

After a moment other members raised their hands to volunteer. Jenna felt proud—she was in charge of setting up and making the soup. *It's going to be fun*, she thought.

Mr. Tam glanced at his watch. "I'm sorry, but I have to leave now." He handed Marissa the paper with the names. "You finish filling out the jobs list," he said, "and I'll see all of you same time next week."

As soon as he was out the door, Marissa let out a happy whoop. "I thought he'd never leave!" She put the paper down on a table. "Who wants to be in charge of decorations?" she asked.

"Me!" said Wendy. "I've got a really cool idea."

"But—what about the rest of the menu?" asked Jenna. "All we have so far is soup, salad, and dessert."

"Maybe that's all they'll want to eat," joked Marissa. "My grandma doesn't eat a lot. Don't worry about it."

"I thought silver and gold would be nice," Wendy went on. "It would match the dress my parents sent me for my birthday. We could make streamers and flowers."

"Talking about dresses," said one of the girls Jenna didn't know. "Did anyone see the way Toby Milgram was dressed today?"

"She looked like a blimp!" said Wendy hysterically.

"No, she looked like a meatloaf," Del insisted.

James stood up and pretended to be a walking meatloaf, and Marissa and the others fell down laughing. Jenna and Danny exchanged confused looks and shrugs. *Was this what the Shadow Club was really all about?*

Later that evening Jenna was sitting at the desk in her tiny single room, working on her homework. For once she wished she had a roommate, someone she could ask to help her with math problems. She yawned and stretched, then settled back to concentrate on the book. The problem on the page in front of her seemed to swim before her tired eyes.

A sound like tapping startled her. It wasn't coming from the door, though. It was coming from the window.

That's weird, Jenna thought. *No one could be tapping on my window. I'm on the second floor! Maybe it's raining.* She opened the curtains and peeked out. The sky was cloudy, with no sign of rain. In fact, tiny white snowflakes were falling. It seemed early for snow after all the unusually warm weather. *Can snowflakes make a tapping sound?* she wondered.

She turned away from the window to search for her nightgown. The sound came again.

Tap . . . tap . . . tap.

"What in the world?" Jenna went back to the window. Snowflakes were still swirling above the pine trees. She closed the curtain, shrugged, then started to put away her books and papers. *Maybe I imagined it,* she thought.

Tap. Tap . . . tap . . . tap.

Alarmed, she went back to the window and peered out again. The light snow had started to stick, blanketing the lawn with feathery whiteness. Jenna's eye was caught by a sudden movement.

There, at the edge of the lawn, a dark figure was going into the woods. In its hands, the figure held a pickax. It stopped and turned back toward the academy. Jenna felt herself go stiff with terror. The figure had no head.

Chapter 7

Jenna held her breath as the headless figure continued to stand at the edge of the woods.

Could it be true? she wondered. *Could that really be Jeb Bendigo's ghost?* Without warning the figure disappeared into the woods. Surprised, Jenna saw a trail of footprints in the snow.

Her heart pounding, she closed the curtain and sat on her bed. *Wait a minute,* she thought. *Ghosts don't leave footprints.* She laughed and then just as quickly stopped. *If it's not a ghost, then it's someone trying to scare me—someone who knows I went to Bendigo's cabin. The question is, who and why?*

Jenna walked around her room, trying to figure out the mystery of the headless figure. Could it be the members of the Shadow Club still giving her a hard time? That didn't really make sense, but then seeing a headless figure out her window didn't make sense either.

At last Jenna gave up on the mystery. No longer sleepy, she decided to work on biology. She had to write up a report on the lab work she'd done that afternoon. As she looked through her papers, she realized she'd left all her lab form sheets in the biology lab.

She knew Jeff always had a lot of lab forms and decided to borrow one from him. She went to his room. The door was half open. "Jeff?" she called. "Rob?" She knocked once, then walked into the room. The light was on, but no one was there. Jeff's desk was neat and organized, his books between a pair of bookends and his notebooks stacked to one side. It took only a few moments to find a folder full of blank lab forms. She took one out and was about to leave when her eye caught Rob's desk.

Even if she hadn't known Rob shared the room, she would have been able to figure out which study area was his. It was as messy as Jeff's was neat. Piles of books covered most of the floor and nearly all of the desk. Papers and pens were sticking out at strange angles. A large book lay open on the very edge of the desk. Jenna went over and pushed the book into the center of the desk so it wouldn't fall. And then she saw the picture on the open page of the book. It was a drawing of an old mining camp. In one corner of the picture was the figure of a headless ghost.

Her heart beating faster, Jenna looked at the title of

the book: *Legends of Phantom Valley*. She turned back to the open page and saw that Rob had been reading about the legend of Jeb Bendigo. *Why in the world is Rob reading this?* she wondered. *He says all those stories are silly.* She scanned the page and felt the hair on the back of her neck rise. She decided to read the entry slowly.

Jenna was concentrating so hard that she wasn't aware of anything until the door to the room slammed shut.

"What are you doing here?" Rob demanded angrily.

Jenna didn't know what to say. She still remembered when her mom married his dad and their two families had moved in together. Rob had warned her then: "I hate people who snoop through my stuff."

"Well?" He wasn't going to let her off the hook. "I want to know what you were doing reading things on my desk."

"I—I came to borrow some lab forms from Jeff."

"Jeff's desk is over there," Rob pointed out. "So why are you snooping around my stuff?"

"I'm not snooping!" Jenna felt herself getting angry. "I told you, I came here to see Jeff. This book was falling off your desk, and I was putting it back and—" She hesitated. "It looked interesting, that's all. You don't have to throw a fit."

Rob glared at her. "You've got two seconds to get out of this room."

"Don't worry, I'm leaving." Jenna went to the door.

She glanced back at her stepbrother, but he was still glaring at her as if they were enemies. She left without another word.

"Today," said Mr. Rothrock, the biology teacher, "we're going to do something a little different. Instead of a pop quiz on pond life, we're going to have a contest."

Some of the kids groaned, including Jenna. Behind her, she heard Jeff whisper, "Great." He was serious! Jeff loved contests—anything that gave him a chance to win.

"Everyone stand up, please," Mr. Rothrock went on. "I am going to show each of you a picture of something related to pond life. Then I'll ask each of you a question about that picture. If you get the answer wrong, you sit down. If you remain standing to the end and win, I'll add an extra-credit A to your grade-point average. Is that clear?"

Jenna listened to the rules with a sinking feeling. Biology was her worst subject. She'd been studying like mad lately, but still she wasn't great at it and didn't want to be quizzed in front of the entire class.

The contest began. To Jenna's surprise, she knew the answers to all of her questions. After twenty minutes she and Jeff were the only students standing.

"I can see you've both been doing your homework," said a pleased Mr. Rothrock. He held up a picture of a strange-looking black and white reptile. "Jeff, what's the name of this creature?"

Jeff looked at the picture, then said, "It's a lizard." Even Jenna had to admit it looked like a lizard.

"I'm sorry, Jeff," Mr. Rothrock said. "You'll have to sit down." Some of the class members laughed, and Jenna could see Jeff's face growing red.

"Jenna," said the teacher, "do you know what kind of creature this is?"

Jenna studied the picture a moment, thinking hard. And then she remembered reading about this animal in the textbook. "I think that's a salamander," she said.

"Good work!" said Mr. Rothrock, smiling. "We have our winner, and you have an extra-credit A on your record!"

Feeling pleased, Jenna sat down. She turned around, to wish Jeff better luck next time. To her surprise, he had a look of hatred on his face. "You think you're so great," he whispered. "You get whatever you want. But I've got news for you, Jenna Black. You're not so great. I'll show you. Just you wait. . . ."

For a moment Jenna felt as if she'd been slapped. "What's your problem?" she hissed back. "It was just a silly contest."

Jeff didn't answer except to say, "You wait and see. You just wait and see."

That evening Jenna and Deidre met in the library to work on their biology term papers. Jenna was writing about wild food plants growing in the Phantom Valley area. She already had a stack of books picked out.

"I've got an article on southwestern herbs if you need it," Deidre said.

"Thanks," Jenna said gratefully. After what had happened with Rob and Jeff, she was beginning to wonder if everyone hated her.

The girls worked silently for about an hour and then agreed to take a ten-minute break. "How are things going with the Shadow Club?" Deidre asked as they walked outside.

"Well, we've had a meeting about the senior citizens' dinner," Jenna answered. "I'm in charge of setting the tables and cooking the first course for the dinner."

"Really?" said Deidre. "That sounds neat. Can someone who isn't a member of the club help?"

"Well, sure," said Jenna. "Do you really want to?"

"Of course I do," said Deidre. "I wish I'd made it into the club, but I guess helping out is the next best thing."

Jenna smiled. She was glad that Deidre had become her friend.

"So what's it like being one of them?" Deidre asked. "Are Marissa and Wendy any nicer?"

"Not exactly," Jenna said. "Actually, I'm beginning to wonder if they aren't still putting me through tests."

"You're in," said Deidre. "Why would they do that?"

"I don't know," Jenna admitted. "And I'm not even sure they are. Nothing's happened for a couple of days."

"What *did* happen?"

Jenna took a deep breath and wondered if Deidre would think she was crazy. "The other night I saw the headless ghost again."

"Where?" asked Deidre, sounding alarmed.

"Outside my window," said Jenna. "On the lawn. It was no big deal. Maybe the club's still giving me a hard time because I'm a new member. I'm sure they'll stop soon."

"Are you sure it's the Shadow Club?" asked Deidre.

"Well, of course," said Jenna. "I mean, it couldn't really be a ghost."

Deidre shrugged. "We all know strange things happen in Phantom Valley."

"Well, ghosts don't leave footprints," Jenna said.

Deidre's eyes widened. "It left footprints?"

"Yes, in the snow," said Jenna. "That's why I know it was a person and not a ghost."

"I don't want to scare you," said Deidre. "But one of the legends about the ghost of Jeb Bendigo is that not only does he have a pickax, but he carries his fool's gold around with him. Supposedly, it makes him so heavy that he leaves footprints."

Chapter 8

Two nights later Jenna was curled up on her bed, doing her English homework. A knock on her door startled her. "Who is it?" she called.

"It's Rob."

Jenna put the book down and took a deep breath. She and Rob hadn't spoken since that bad scene in his room. She wasn't sure she wanted to talk to him now, either.

Rob knocked again. "I need to talk to you. It will only take a minute."

Jenna sighed, then opened the door. "I wasn't snooping," she said, eying him.

"I know," Rob agreed. "I'm sorry."

Jenna felt her anger begin to fade.

"Okay," Jenna said. "But because you were so mean, you now owe me a favor."

56

"What's that?"

"The Shadow Club could use some help serving dinner for the retirement home in two days. Think you could help out?"

Rob studied the ceiling. "Only if you help me study for my math test."

Jenna smiled. "Deal."

Two days later Jenna was standing in the home ec kitchen, slicing mushrooms for her favorite vegetable soup on a wooden cutting board. The potatoes, onions, carrots, and tomatoes were already cooking in a big pot on the stove. The dinner for the Silverbell Retirement Home would be held that evening in the teachers' dining room.

"Help is here," said Deidre, entering the room with an armful of groceries. "Just put me to work."

"Great," said Jenna. "Do you want to make a salad?"

"No problem." Deidre took in the empty kitchen. "Are you cooking this dinner by yourself?" she asked. "What happened to the rest of the Shadow Club?"

"Marissa, Wendy, and Tamara are all putting up the decorations," Jenna said. "The others will be here later to cook, and believe it or not, both Rob and Jeff said they'd help serve." She glanced at her watch. "Oh, no, I told Rob I'd help him study a little more for his math test, in exchange for his working tonight. The only problem is, I forgot I'd be cooking this afternoon."

"Go ahead," Deidre said. "I'll keep an eye on your soup."

"Thanks," Jenna said. "It shouldn't take that long."

Jenna hurried to her dorm room, where Rob was supposed to meet her. He wasn't there. Thirty-five minutes later there was still no sign of Rob. *Great*, she thought. *This is always how Rob acts. Unless he thought I was supposed to meet him in his room.* She decided to check the boys' room, but no one was there either.

Why had Rob asked her for help if he didn't plan to study? It seemed as if he was always looking for trouble. Jenna glanced at her watch. She'd just wasted nearly an hour. *Fine*, she thought. *Let him study on his own.*

She started back toward the home ec kitchen in the classroom annex. The sun was setting, and a brisk wind had picked up. In half an hour the people were to arrive for dinner. Jenna knew that if Rob had forgotten about their study session, he would also forget to help serve at the dinner.

As Jenna passed the gym, she heard the sound of a basketball being bounced. On a hunch, she poked her head inside. Sure enough, there was Rob, sinking baskets.

"Rob!" she said angrily. "We were supposed to study geometry, remember?"

"What time is it?" he asked, checking his watch. "Oops! I didn't realize it was so late. How about if we study now?"

"We can't. I've got to finish the dinner for tonight. And, in case you don't remember, you promised to help."

"No problem," Rob said. "You know, Jenna, you get all excited over nothing."

Jenna just folded her arms and glared at him.

"All right, all right," he said. "I'll help now."

Jenna followed Rob back across the gym toward the outside door. As he reached up to turn out the light there was a sudden banging noise and the door to the gym slammed shut.

"What was that?" asked Rob.

"The door to the outside must have blown shut," said Jenna. "It's really windy out."

She turned the knob. The door wouldn't open.

"Let me try." Rob pushed as hard as he could, but the door was stuck. "It feels as if it's locked from the outside," he said, sounding puzzled. "The hall door is always locked at this time," he added.

"Great," said Jenna. "The senior citizens will be coming to dinner soon, and I'm stuck in the gym. What about the locker rooms?"

"Locked," he replied. "Maybe we can go out through a window," Rob suggested. He went to a window and opened the lock. Then he stepped back, horror on his face.

"What's wrong?" Jenna asked.

"I—I don't know," he answered. "I thought I saw—"

"What?" Jenna ran to the window and peered out into the darkness. At first all she saw were the shadows of trees.

Then she saw it. Something was moving toward the building. It was the headless figure, and in its hand was a pickax. It was running straight for her!

"No," she cried, stumbling backward.

She felt Rob's hand on her shoulder. "Are we imagining this?" he asked.

Jenna shook her head.

Rob swore under his breath. "Let's get out of here. *Now!*"

Jenna, though, stood frozen, staring at the headless figure with the pickax in its hand. Now, it was just outside the window. Jenna watched as it slowly raised the ax.

"Get down!" Rob cried, pulling her away from the window. "We've got to find a way out of here!"

Then Jenna heard a sharp *crack*, and the glass in the window cracked in a spider web pattern.

"It's going to get us!" Rob shouted. He grabbed Jenna's hand, and they ran to the outside door. Rob hurled himself against it. The door still didn't budge.

Jenna turned and saw the ax smash against the window a second time. She felt herself start to shake. The ax would strike again, she knew. And when it did, the safety glass would break.

"Come on," Rob said, "we can hide under the bleachers."

They never made it that far. The doors to the gym suddenly burst wide open.

Chapter 9

Jenna screamed as the cold air rushed into the gym, and a tall, dark figure strode in through the door. Jenna saw the surprised face of Mr. Fernandez, the night guard.

"What are you two doing in here?" he asked. "I heard a lot of thumping and banging on the door."

"The door was stuck," said Rob. "But everything's okay now."

"No, it's not," Jenna said. "There's someone or some*thing* out there with a pickax." She pointed to the cracked window. "Look what it just did."

Mr. Fernandez peered at the window and shook his head. "That window's been like that for weeks now."

"But I saw it with my own two eyes," Jenna insisted.

"You must have imagined it," Mr. Fernandez said. "Someone's supposed to come in and fix it this week." He looked at her more carefully. "Are you sure you're all right?"

"We're fine," Rob said.

"Well, you'd better get on out," the guard said. "I've got to lock up."

Jenna and Rob stepped out onto the path. Jenna's knees were still shaky.

"Do you think it's still around here?" Rob asked nervously.

"I don't know," Jenna said, "but why didn't you tell Mr. Fernandez you saw it, too? He thought I was crazy."

Rob looked down at the ground. "You saw how he acted when you told him. Anyway, I've always thought ghost stories were dumb and anyone who believed them was even dumber. Maybe I *didn't* see anything. Maybe it was just shadows."

"You don't really believe that?" Jenna asked.

"After our meeting at the Shadow Club, I wondered why so many people believe that stuff," Rob said. "So I took some books out of the library. And I talked to some of the kids who say they've seen ghosts and spirits. And—and I think there might be something to it."

"So you *do* believe we just saw a ghost."

Her stepbrother ran a hand through his dark blond hair. "What I believe, Jenna, is a lot worse than that.

I think we saw Jeb Bendigo's ghost." He paused, then said, "And I think he's after you."

When Jenna and Rob arrived at the home ec kitchen, the room was packed. From what Jenna could see, nearly everyone she knew was there. The entire Shadow Club and most of their friends were in the kitchen, putting the finishing touches on the meal.

Jenna had only gotten halfway across the room when she heard Deidre's voice behind her. "Where were you? I went to look for you, but couldn't find you anywhere. The soup is done."

Jenna nodded toward her stepbrother. "It took me a long time to find him."

Deidre smiled at Rob. "Welcome. You've got lots of company."

Everyone was talking and laughing as they worked. Jenna felt herself starting to relax and join in the fun. The ghost was far from her mind. "How's the soup?" she asked Deidre.

"Yummy," Deidre replied.

"Perfect," Jenna agreed, taking a taste. She turned to Rob. "Let's see what else needs to be done."

"Uh—sorry, Jen, but I don't think I can stay. I—I don't feel so good after what happened," Rob said. "I think I'd better go back to my room."

Jenna held back her anger. It was just like Rob to back out on helping her. He *did* look kind of queasy, though. "All right," she said. "I'll catch you later."

Jenna went to the teachers' dining room, where the meal was to be served. Jeff was there setting up the last tables, while Wendy and Marissa put out plates and silverware.

"You're late," said Marissa, sounding annoyed.

Jenna didn't bother to answer. Instead, she helped Jeff. She was checking to make sure that everything was where it should be, when the van carrying the senior citizens arrived. *Time to bring on the food*, she thought, going back to the kitchen for her soup.

She'd started to pick up the heavy pot when Jeff appeared in the doorway. "Here, let me take that," he offered.

"Thanks," Jenna said, trying not to sound as surprised as she felt. This was the first time since he hadn't made the club that Jeff was acting nice. She followed him back to the teachers' dining room, and watched him set the soup on the serving table.

Jenna gazed out at the room filled with senior citizens and Chilleen teachers. All the guests were smiling and talking, happy to be at the dinner. Jenna felt proud. *This is why I wanted to be in the club*, she thought. *And ghosts or no ghosts, it's worth it.*

She began ladling the soup out into bowls while Deidre, Jeff, and Cissy brought them to the tables. When the last bowl of soup had been served, Mrs. Danita welcomed everyone and thanked the club.

THE HEADLESS GHOST

Jenna smiled as a handsome white-haired man sneaked a big spoonful of the soup. She watched as he swallowed, hoping he'd like it.

Suddenly the man's face turned bright red and his hands went to his throat. He made a strange, gurgling noise and jumped up from his place, knocking over his chair.

"Help!" he gasped. "Poison!"

Chapter 10

"**I**'ve been poisoned!" the old man screamed.

Jenna watched horrified as he fell to the floor, twisting and kicking. The dining room was deathly silent.

"Call an ambulance!" someone shouted, breaking the silence.

"No one else touch the soup!" Mrs. Danita called, rushing over to the man. A moment later Mrs. Albert, the nurse, came running into the dining room.

"Get back!" she ordered the people gathered around the man. "Give him air!" She leaned down and loosened his collar while they waited for the ambulance.

"How could this happen?" Wendy cried.

Marissa pulled Jenna aside. "You cooked the soup," she said accusingly. "What did you do to it?"

"I don't know," Jenna replied. "I tasted it just before—"

"Everyone calm down," Mrs. Albert suddenly said. "I don't think it's poison."

A moment later the old man sat up. "I think I'll be all right," he said.

"Just stay quiet," said Mrs. Albert. "You still need to be checked out."

By the time the ambulance came, the old man was sitting in a chair and joking, feeling much better. "Let's take a look at that soup," said one of the paramedics. She took a big spoonful out, and sniffed it. "Doesn't smell like anything but chili peppers," she said. "Where did this come from?"

"I made it in the home ec kitchen," Jenna said, shifting uncomfortably. She knew that everyone in the room was looking at her. "I'll show you."

She led the paramedics, Mrs. Danita, and Mrs. Albert back to the kitchen. Everything looked just the way it was supposed to. The chicken and potatoes made by Danny and Del sat on a table, ready to be served.

"What's this?" asked the paramedic. She ran her finger over the top of the stove. Her finger came away with small red and yellow flecks on it. "Is this where you cooked the soup?"

"Yes, it was that burner," said Jenna, pointing. Now she saw flecks all around the burner, too. They looked like . . . Jenna ran to the spice rack. The lid to the big jar of red-hot chili pepper flakes was off. The jar was empty.

The paramedic laughed. "Looks like someone overdid it on the chili peppers."

"But how could that have happened?" asked Mrs. Danita.

"Must have been someone's idea of a joke," said the paramedic. "You're lucky that's all it was."

"I don't understand," said Jenna. "I tasted the soup just before I checked the tables. It was fine," she insisted.

"I'm going to see that this matter is looked into," said Mrs. Danita. She took a taste of the chicken and potatoes. "This tastes fine," she said. "Jenna, will you please keep an eye on these dishes till the other members of the club can serve them?"

Feeling numb, Jenna watched Mrs. Danita and the others leave. *Who could have done it?* she asked herself. Anyone, really. There were so many people working in the kitchen, just about anyone could have dumped the chili pepper into the soup. But how could they do it without being seen? How could anyone, except a ghost . . .

"I don't believe this!" Jenna turned to see Marissa's angry face in the doorway. "How could you let this happen?" the girl demanded.

"I don't know," Jenna said miserably. "I don't know how it happened."

"It could have ruined the whole dinner," added Wendy. "Are you *trying* to get the Shadow Club in trouble?"

"I'm sorry," Jenna said. "I just don't know what happened. I'm sorry."

"We'll talk about it again later," said Marissa. "Now, come on, Wendy, let's serve the main course." She and Wendy took the chicken and potatoes to the dining room. Jenna didn't feel like going with them. She didn't want to see the other kids or the guests.

To keep her mind off what had happened, she started cleaning up the spilled peppers. First she wiped the stove, then started taking all the jars and bottles out of the spice rack. When she put the oregano back, it wouldn't fit. *There must be something stuck behind it,* Jenna thought. She removed the jar and reached her hand back in the shelf. Her fingers touched something hard. She pulled it out and gasped.

Sitting in the palm of her hand was a tiny lump of fool's gold.

The next morning Jenna went down to breakfast as soon as the dining room opened. There were only a few kids there that early, which was just fine with her. She knew everyone would be talking about the "poisoned" soup.

She was eating her oatmeal, trying to figure out what to do next, when Rob sat down across from her.

"What are you doing up so early?" Jenna asked. "Usually you're the last one to breakfast."

"I couldn't sleep," said Rob. "I can't get out of my mind what happened last night in the gym."

"The gym?" For a moment Jenna didn't know what he meant. "Oh," she said. "You mean the thing we saw."

"The *ghost*," said Rob. "The headless ghost. Did you forget?"

"It's just that something much worse happened later," Jenna said. Quickly she told Rob about the soup. When she finished, he seemed to be frightened, the way he had been in the gym.

"You were really lucky," he said, his voice shaking. "Do you realize that it could have been real poison?"

"Who would want to poison some harmless senior citizens?"

"It's not a 'who,' it's a *what*."

Jenna shut her eyes. "Please tell me you're not going to start talking about the ghost again."

"We both saw it!" Rob said. "And who else could have ruined the soup?"

"But why would a ghost want to mess up soup?" Jenna asked. She almost laughed, the idea was so funny.

"That's not why he did it," said Rob. "Don't you see? It was a warning. He was showing you how close he can get—any time he wants—to you, and anyone around you," he added, his face pale.

"So what do I do about it?"

Rob gave a low, shaky laugh. "Get yourself into another school, maybe. One that's far from here. I'm calling home. I'm going to tell them to come get us."

"Are you crazy?" said Jenna. "We can't just leave. I mean, it's the middle of the year."

"So what?" said Rob. "Which is more important—finishing the school year, or saving your life?"

Jenna rolled her eyes. "I know you never liked Chilleen, but—"

"I'm not kidding," Rob broke in. "Everything I've read says Jeb Bendigo's ghost has killed before. Do you want to be next?"

It was nearly time for lights-out when Jenna left the library that night. It had been a while since she'd worked on her biology paper, and she had to do extra that night.

The academy was almost dark as Jenna crossed the lobby to the other wing where her dorm room was. Her mind was still on her paper. She'd finished the research and a good chunk of the writing. It was actually coming together better than she'd hoped.

She started up the stairs to her room, still thinking about her project. Then, without warning, the stairway light clicked off.

"Whoa!" Jenna said out loud, figuring the lightbulb had blown out. She held on to the rail and made her way in the dark up to her floor. She was just about to turn toward her room when something hit her hard on the shoulder. Before she could grab for the railing, she felt herself falling—falling straight down the steep stairs.

Chapter 11

"**N**o!" Jenna screamed as she grabbed at the bannister. Her hand caught one of its rungs, and a moment later she stopped in a heap on the stairs. Her leg was twisted beneath her, and a sudden, sharp pain shot through her ankle.

Jenna winced and looked up toward the landing, where she had been pushed. No one was there. She was about to call for help when the light clicked on.

"Jenna!" It was Mrs. Danita, sounding upset. "What happened? Are you all right?" The headmistress rushed up the stairs and knelt beside Jenna. "Don't try to move," she said. "I'll call the—"

"I'm all right," said Jenna. She knew she didn't sound all right, though.

"Let me see." Gently, Mrs. Danita touched Jenna's

ankle. "It's starting to swell," she said. "I'd better call the nurse."

While they waited for Mrs. Albert to come, Mrs. Danita asked Jenna what had happened.

"I . . . I was going up the stairs," Jenna said. "Suddenly the lights went out. The next thing I knew, someone hit me and pushed me down the stairs."

"Someone pushed you?" Mrs. Danita sounded uncertain. "Are you sure about that?"

"I felt it," Jenna said. "Someone hit me on the shoulder and then pushed me."

"Did you see anyone?" the headmistress asked.

"The light was out."

"I understand how upset you are, but maybe you tripped," Mrs. Danita said. "Besides, who would want to harm you? And why? That's a very serious charge to make, Jenna. I think you may just be remembering it wrong."

"Maybe," said Jenna, blinking back some tears. She knew Mrs. Danita didn't believe her.

Then Mrs. Albert arrived and examined Jenna's ankle. "I think it's just a sprain," the nurse said. "But we'll get an X ray in Silverbell tomorrow. For tonight, let's get you upstairs and put some ice on it."

The two women helped Jenna up the stairs. When they got to the landing where she had been pushed— or thought she had been pushed—Mrs. Danita stopped suddenly.

"What's this?" she said, leaning over to pick something up. Jenna looked at the object the headmistress was holding in her hand.

"It looks like a piece of fool's gold," said the nurse, sounding surprised. "How did it get here?"

"I can't imagine," said Mrs. Danita. "Maybe—"

Jenna had stopped listening. *The ghost—again! This has gone too far*, she thought.

"Jenna?" said Mrs. Danita.

Jenna realized Mrs. Danita was asking her something. "What, Mrs. Danita?"

"I said, did you see this piece of rock before?"

For a moment Jenna thought about telling the headmistress everything that had been happening. Then she realized she couldn't. Mrs. Danita probably wouldn't believe her, and she had sworn never to give away the secrets of the Shadow Club. She was in serious trouble, and there was no one who could help her.

Jenna limped out of the school van the next morning with an elastic bandage wrapped around her ankle and an aluminum crutch under her right arm. The hospital in Silverbell had x-rayed her ankle and found that it was only a sprain. "Keep it bandaged and try to stay off it as much as possible," the doctor had said.

All that day Jenna reviewed what had happened the night before. *Was it a ghost or a human who had pushed her?* she wondered. She finally decided that it was a human hand that had pushed her. The idea of a ghost was just too scary. If her enemy was a person, who was it? Because of the fool's gold, it had to be someone connected with the Shadow Club, she thought.

Jenna decided that it was time she and Marissa had a talk. She had to find out if the Shadow Club had any part in the strange things that were happening to her. Marissa wasn't in any of her classes, though, and thanks to her ankle, Jenna couldn't search for the older girl.

After her last class, Jenna went back to her room to work on her biology paper, which was due the next day. By dinner time she was nearly finished. All that she had left to write was the ending. After eating, she'd finish up and then get a good night's sleep.

By the time Jenna got to the dining room, nearly everyone was through the dinner line. She was at the dessert table when Deidre came up to her, staring at the crutch. "Jenna, what happened to you?"

"Oh, right, I guess I didn't see you today," said Jenna. "I had a little accident last night."

"It looks like more than a little accident!" said Deidre, taking Jenna's tray from her. "Let me help you to a table."

"Have you seen Marissa?" Jenna asked when they were seated. "I need to talk to her."

"She was here earlier," said Deidre. "But I think she went off to study with Tamara. Tell me what happened," her friend said, concerned.

"I—well, I fell down a couple of stairs," Jenna said. She had told about a hundred people and felt a little embarrassed each time.

"What do you mean you fell down a couple of stairs? Did you slip?"

"Not exactly," said Jenna. Except for Mrs. Danita, she hadn't told anyone what had really happened. She decided she could confide in Deidre. "I didn't really slip," she said. "I—I was pushed. Or at least that's what it felt like."

Deidre's face became white. "Who pushed you?"

"I don't know," said Jenna. "I'm not even sure if it really happened." Still feeling a little embarrassed, she told Deidre the whole story, ending with finding the piece of fool's gold on the landing.

For a long time Deidre didn't say anything. When she finally spoke her voice was shaky. "Are you sure about this?"

"I know what happened," said Jenna. "But maybe it wasn't that big a deal. In fact, I think it may be the Shadow Club, still playing tricks. Or maybe they're just paying me back for the soup disaster."

"That's not what it is," said Deidre. She sounded very sure. "It's—oh, Jenna, I don't know how to tell you this, but it was the ghost. That's why you didn't see anyone."

Jenna just stared at her friend. "How can you be sure?" she asked. "I mean, it's true I didn't see anyone, but—"

"I'm totally serious!" Deidre insisted. "My father has told me all about Jeb Bendigo. Jeb's after you, Jenna. It's because you took his gold. He's after you the way he went after that boy twenty years ago!"

"That's just superstition," Jenna told Deidre. "There isn't really a—"

"Then how did the fool's gold get on the landing? And how come you felt someone push you? If it was a joke, why didn't you see anyone?"

"I don't know," Jenna admitted. "But I'm not going to make myself crazy trying to figure it out. Don't worry about me, Deidre. Everything's going to be fine."

On the way back to her room Jenna wondered if the ghost of Jeb Bendigo could really be after her. Somehow, though, she was sure that someone human was trying to scare her—either someone already in the Shadow Club or someone who had wanted to get in. Ever since she had joined, though, most of the members had been really nice to her—except for Marissa and Wendy. They still acted like snobs, but they acted that way to most of the school.

Jenna reached the stairs to her room and started up slowly, using the crutch. She stopped every step or two to rest and look around. *Don't get nervous*, she told herself.

On the second-floor landing she almost bumped into Jeff. "Hey!" he exclaimed. "Watch where you're going."

"I was!" Jenna shot back. "You're the one who should be careful."

"Yeah, yeah," he said. "I hear you sprained your

ankle." He didn't say he was sorry about her accident, though. Instead he asked, "You been working on your bio paper?"

"It's getting there," she answered, starting to move past him.

"Oh, really?" said Jeff, blocking her way. "Do you mean you've actually been able to take enough time from your spooky little club to work on it?"

"For your information," said Jenna, "all I have left to write is the ending."

"Well, mine's all done," said Jeff, smirking at her.

By the time Jenna got to her room, she was fuming. For some reason Jeff seemed to think it was her fault that he didn't get into the Shadow Club. *If I'd known it was going to lead to this much trouble . . .* she thought. And yet she still wanted to be part of it. Being in the Shadow Club hadn't made her instantly popular, but it did make her feel special.

She opened the door to her room, switched on the light, and leaned her crutch against the wall. She started to hop over to her desk and then stopped, shocked. The floor of her room was covered with tiny flecks of white.

What in the world? Jenna wondered. Then, instantly, she knew what the white flecks were. They were ripped-up pieces of paper. Hundreds of torn pieces of paper, covering every surface.

In rising panic Jenna hobbled over to her desk, where

she kept her notebooks. Every page in every one of her notebooks had been torn out and ripped into tiny pieces. She frantically searched for her biology term paper. There was no sign of it. And then she saw a long, jagged scrap of paper on her study chair. Her hands shaking, she picked it up. It was all that was left of the first page of the term paper.

Chapter 12

"Someone broke into my room," Jenna said aloud, as if by saying it she could make herself believe it. "Someone broke into my room and tore everything apart, including the term paper I've been working on for weeks."

The whole room started to go blurry as tears came to her eyes. If she didn't turn the term paper in, she'd get on the D list in biology. And if that happened, she would have to drop out of the Shadow Club.

Jenna grabbed a tissue and sat down on the bed. Who would have broken into her room? she wondered. The only answer she could come up with was Jeff. Jenna knew that since she had won the contest in class, her grade in biology was higher than Jeff's. The only way Jeff could end the semester with a higher grade was if she couldn't hand in her term paper.

THE HEADLESS GHOST

Still, she didn't think Jeff would go so far as to break into her room and destroy her paper. Her thoughts turned to Marissa. The club president had pulled several cruel pranks already. Now that Jenna was in the Shadow Club, Marissa was still just as mean as she had been before.

Jenna shivered as a sudden breeze swept through the room. *That's strange*, she thought. *I'm sure I left the window closed.* She hobbled over to the window, started to pull it down, and then stopped. There, sitting on the windowsill, glittering in the moonlight, was a cube of fool's gold.

She held the shiny metal in her hand, feeling a wave of anger spread through her body. *Someone is trying to scare me*, she thought. *And I'm going to find out who.*

Picking up her crutch, she hobbled down the hall to Marissa's room at the end of the wing.

She knocked on the door and then heard Marissa call out, "It's open. Come on in."

Jenna pushed the door open. Marissa was sitting cross-legged on her bed, polishing her fingernails. Her eyes took in Jenna's bandage and the crutch. "What happened to you?" she asked.

"As if you didn't know," said Jenna.

"Huh," Marissa said absently.

"It's just lucky I didn't break my leg," Jenna went on. "A sprained ankle's bad enough. But tonight—breaking into my room and tearing up my term paper . . . You guys went too far. Why are you doing all this to me? When are the tests going to stop?"

"What *are* you talking about?" Marissa asked.

"Don't pretend you don't know," Jenna said. "I've seen what a good actress you are. I always wanted to be in the Shadow Club. I wanted it more than anything. But I—I can't take this anymore."

"Jenna," Marissa said, "don't you know that all the tests stop as soon as someone makes the club?"

Maybe, Jenna thought. "But you're still mad about the senior citizens' dinner," Jenna said.

Marissa blew on her nails. "Well, poisoning people isn't great."

"So you're haunting me with a headless ghost."

Marissa yawned. "Why don't you sit down and tell me what happened, since it sounds like you're going to anyway."

Jenna sat down on Marissa's roommate's bed and began to tell her everything. "And then tonight," she finished, "I got back to my room and found someone had broken in. All my school papers were trashed. My term paper that I've been working on was torn into little pieces. And I found this." She held out the piece of fool's gold.

Marissa, who had been acting bored, suddenly became alarmed. "Where exactly did you find this?" she asked, her voice almost a whisper.

"I told you," said Jenna. "It was on my windowsill."

"I don't believe it," said Marissa.

"What do you mean? Didn't you put it there?"

"I told you the Shadow Club has nothing to do with

82

what's been happening," Marissa said. "But, Jenna—the things you've said are happening—they're the exact same things that happened to the kid who was killed twenty years ago."

Jenna felt her heart begin to pound.

"We didn't tell the pledges too much about it," Marissa went on. "But right after the kid went into Jeb Bendigo's cabin, strange things started to happen to him."

"Like what?"

"The kinds of things you've been talking about," Marissa answered. "He kept seeing the headless ghost outside his room. His school books and papers disappeared. And one night—one night he was pushed down the stairs. He was almost killed."

"Who did those things to him?"

"No one knew for sure. But—but everyone thought it was the ghost of Jeb Bendigo."

"Well, I don't believe in ghosts," said Jenna.

"I haven't told you the worst thing yet," said Marissa. She took a deep breath and went on. "Like how he finally got killed. It was at the winter party, the biggest party of the year for the club. It was cold, and he went outside to get some wood for the fire. Only he never came back.

"They found him four days later buried in the snow, his neck broken. It could have been an accident. Only—only there was a little pile of fool's gold lying right by his head."

Marissa's face was white. "I'm beginning to think we shouldn't have sent you to the cabin. This is getting to be too much like what happened before."

Jenna thought about what Marissa said and then shrugged. "I don't know what to believe anymore. But if it really is a ghost, what do I do?"

"I don't know what to tell you," Marissa said. "If it is Bendigo's ghost, there isn't anything that will stop him."

Chapter 13

As Jenna walked along the forest path, her boots squeaked in the new snow. The big, wet flakes were coming down so thick and fast she could barely see the trees. Usually Jenna loved snow. Today, it seemed little more than a reason to wear boots.

She was on her way to the Shadow Club's winter party at the lodge. She should have been excited, she knew. Every year the club had the winter party, and it was the biggest event of the whole year. The other members had been talking about it for days now.

Somehow, though, Jenna just couldn't get in the mood. About the only good things that had happened in the past two weeks were that her ankle had healed, and that Mr. Rothrock had given her extra time to rewrite her biology term paper. Marissa and Wendy were still unfriendly and Jeff was still being mean to her.

Even though nothing strange had happened since the night her room was broken into, Rob still thought that they should leave Chilleen before something worse happened.

She tried to cheer up as the lodge came into sight, a soft-edged shape draped in thick snow. White smoke curled out of the chimney. Jenna opened the door and could hear the music and laughter.

"Hey, look who's here," said Del with a big smile. "It's our new member."

"Hi, Jenna," said Marissa in a friendly voice. "Did you bring the chips?"

Jenna handed the club president a plastic bag containing packages of potato and corn chips. She took off her ski jacket and set it by the fire to dry out.

"It's really snowing out there," she said.

"I know," said Wendy. "We were beginning to wonder if you were buried in it."

"Not quite," said Jenna. "But it's getting harder to walk." She went over to the food table and began talking to some of the other kids.

"Want to dance?" James asked, coming up to her.

Jenna didn't really feel like dancing, but she didn't want to let James down. She let him bring her onto the dance floor. After a few minutes the music took over, and Jenna started enjoying herself. She danced with James and then Del and then Dave. Finally, out of breath, she stopped to get a soda. She might have mixed feelings about the Shadow Club, but she had to admit she was having fun.

"Do you know when Mr. Tam's coming?" Tamara asked. "I'm supposed to take the club picture." Tamara was chief photographer for the school yearbook.

"There's some big teachers' meeting this afternoon," said Del. "He said he'll be here after that."

"Well, he'd better hurry up," said Tamara, checking her watch. "It'll be dark soon."

"I don't know how he can get here," said Wendy, rubbing a clean circle on the window to peer out. "It's practically a blizzard out there."

"You're not kidding," said Del. He got up and put on his jacket. "I'm going to check this out."

He disappeared into the whiteness outside. A few minutes later he came back, grinning. His face was bright red from the cold. "Hey, everyone," he shouted. "You'll never guess what."

The others quieted for a moment and Del went on. "We're snowed in!" he announced.

"We're what?" exclaimed Marissa.

"I'm serious," said Del. "I just checked it out. The path to the school is completely covered, and the snow's still falling. I don't think it's going to be safe to go back till it dies down."

"You mean we're going to have to stay here all night?" Wendy asked.

"Looks like it," said Del. "Maybe for the weekend."

A cheer went up. "This is going to be great," James said. "We've got plenty of food, candles, and firewood. Music, too, if the batteries hold out."

Jenna joined the others as they gathered around the fireplace. While Marissa began popping corn in an old-fashioned wire basket over the fire, Del began telling a ghost story.

"This one is true," he began. "My uncle told it to me. It seems that he and some friends were in a cabin up in the mountains. It was about this time of year, and it was snowing really hard. They were all sleeping when there was a sudden thumping noise on the roof of the cabin."

A moment later there was a thumping noise on the roof of the cabin. Everyone laughed. "Hey, Del," said Danny. "How'd you do that?"

"I don't know," said Del, acting surprised. "Anyway—"

There was another thump, this time on the side of the cabin.

"What could that be?" wondered Wendy.

"It must be the wind," said Marissa. "Blowing snow off the trees."

Before Del could continue, the thumping noises grew louder.

"This is weird," said Tamara, sounding scared. "It sounds as if someone's trying to get through the wall."

"Which is impossible," said Marissa. "It's just the—"

Her sentence was cut off by a terrified scream from outside. The other members of the club all silently stared at one another. "That wasn't the wind," whispered Wendy.

Jenna looked carefully from one member of the club to the other. *Was this another trick? A joke to scare the newest members of the club? Or was it—don't let it be Bendigo's ghost,* she prayed.

There was another horrible scream. Then another, much louder one, pierced the air.

Marissa's dark eyes were wide with fear. "Jenna," she said, "It's Jeb Bendigo. He's come for you."

Jenna felt a flash of anger. "Don't be ridic—" Her voice broke as more thumps sounded, this time against the door.

"He followed you here!" Marissa's voice rose in panic. "Jenna stole his treasure and now he wants it back!"

The pounding on the door became louder and louder. Jenna stood, frozen with fear, watching the old wooden door shake.

Abruptly, the pounding stopped. "Let me in!" a horribly inhuman voice cried. "Let me in!"

Chapter 14

The members of the Shadow Club just stood and stared. "Let me in!" the voice cried again. The voice sounded frightened. Frightened—and in trouble.

Jenna checked the leaders of the club. She was waiting for someone to smile, so she'd know it was a joke. No one was smiling. Marissa and Wendy both looked scared to death.

"Who is it?" Del yelled.

There was no answer. They all stared at the door.

The pounding started again. Del started for the door.

"Don't open it!" Wendy shrieked.

"But I want to find out who—"

"All the club members are here!" said Marissa. "Just ignore it!"

"Wait—" said Jenna. "What if it's someone from school? Someone who got lost in the blizzard?"

"Someone who was thumping on the roof?" asked Wendy.

"That could have been the wind," Jenna said. "I'm going to go to the door."

"No!" cried Tamara, grabbing her hand. "What if it's the ghost? What if he's after all of us?"

"Jenna's right," said Del. "It might be someone from school. Someone who needs help."

"All right," said Wendy. "But be careful."

Del nodded. He went over to the big fireplace and took the long metal poker. Then he went to the door. The pounding had stopped, but Jenna thought she could still hear the panicked voice.

Slowly Del opened the door.

The wind came whistling in, bringing a layer of snow with it.

"There's no one there," Del said, sounding puzzled. The other members of the club gathered around, peering out into the swirling whiteness. "This is really weird," continued Del. "Because there are footprints that lead right up to the door."

Footprints, Jenna thought. *Jeb Bendigo's ghost is so weighted down with pyrite that he leaves footprints. What if he really has come for me? I've got to do something.*

Slowly, Jenna walked toward the doorway. A blast of icy air cut through her as she stuck her head out into the storm.

There was no dark headless figure. Her eye was caught by something to the side of the cabin. A small form was lying there, covered with snow.

Jenna and Del rushed to the figure and brushed the snow away. "It's Deidre!" Del said.

"Deidre?" Jenna bent down to help her friend. She touched Deidre's wrist. It felt like ice.

Del turned to Jenna, his eyes dark with sadness. "Jenna, don't," he said. "Go back inside."

Jenna felt her stomach sink. "Why?" she asked Del.

"Just go back inside," he insisted.

Jenna reached for Deidre again, and her friend's cold body seemed stiff.

Chapter 15

"No," Jenna screamed. "Deidre!"

"Get her inside!" someone else called.

Jenna felt a tug on her arm, as someone tried to help her back into the lodge. She stayed where she was, staring at Deidre's pale face. There was a red welt across her forehead. How long had she been out there, pounding on the door, needing their help?

"Come on, Jenna." James put gentle hands on her shoulders and steered her back into the lodge.

"Bring Deidre inside," Marissa ordered. "By the fire!"

"Is she breathing?" asked Tamara.

Del and Danny dragged Deidre's small body over by the fire. For a very long moment she just lay there, not moving. *Please*, Jenna thought. *Please let her be all right.*

As the firelight shone on Deidre, Jenna could finally

see her chest moving. A moment later Deidre's eyelids fluttered, then opened. "Where am I?" she asked.

"Just lie still," Wendy said quietly.

"Get her something to drink," said Del.

Jenna brought Deidre a cup of hot chocolate. "Here," she said gently. "Drink this." She helped her friend sit up, then held the cup of hot liquid to her lips.

Deidre drank the chocolate slowly as she looked around. "It's so warm in here," she said. "Warm and safe."

"What are you doing here?" asked Marissa. "Did you get lost in the storm?"

For a moment Deidre shut her eyes. "I was chased here," she said, her voice shaking. "I was chased by a—a horrible thing without a head."

"What?" asked Marissa.

"The headless ghost?" asked Del.

"The real one," Deidre said. "This time it was the real one."

"What do you mean, this time?" Jenna asked.

"I mean . . . I mean . . ." For a moment Deidre looked as if she was going to cry. "The other times when you saw the headless ghost it was me."

"What?" Jenna couldn't believe her ears.

"Do you mean you were the one who caused Jenna all this trouble?" Marissa asked, suddenly very angry.

"I'm sorry," Deidre said, embarrassed.

"She thought *we* were doing it," Marissa said.

"I know," said Deidre. "I wanted her to think it was the ghost. But somehow I couldn't scare her enough."

"You mean you did all those things?" Jenna asked, angry now.

"Not all," said James, staring at the floor. "The first time you saw the ghost in the woods on the way back from the tests of courage—that was me."

"I did all the rest," Deidre said. "I broke into your room and tore up your term paper. I put the chili peppers in the soup. I scared you in the gym. I—I even pushed you on the stairs."

"You could have really hurt me!" Jenna said.

"I know. I'm sorry," said Deidre. "I only meant to scare you. I didn't want you to fall. And when I saw you fall I got really scared and ran to my room."

Jenna stared at her friend in disbelief. "But why? Why would you do all those things? I thought we were friends. This doesn't make sense."

"I wanted to get even with you," she said in a cold voice.

"For what?" Jenna demanded. "What in the world have I done to you?"

"You know," Deidre said.

"No, I don't," said Jenna.

"You kept me out of the club," Deidre said. "Don't say you didn't. I know you told them."

"Told who? Told them what?" Jenna asked, totally confused.

"That I didn't go into Bendigo's cabin," said Deidre. "That I was scared by the bats."

"That's not true!" Jenna cried. "I never said anything. I promised I wouldn't and I didn't."

"Don't lie," Deidre said, her eyes flashing. "You told them and kept me from making the club—even though you knew how much it meant to me."

"Is that what you think?" Marissa broke in. "You think Jenna told us you didn't fulfill your test of courage?"

"She must have," Deidre said flatly. "Otherwise I would have gotten in."

"It's true you were our top choice," said Marissa. "But Jenna never told us anything. She didn't have to. Del and Wendy followed you to the cabin that night. They saw everything that happened."

"You mean you didn't . . ." Deidre was even more embarrassed now.

"We all knew the truth," Marissa explained. "That was why you didn't get in. It had nothing to do with Jenna."

Deidre looked into the fire. She opened her mouth to say something, then shut it again.

Jenna just stared at Deidre. "Is there more?" she asked. "Is there something else you have against me?"

"No. I just wanted to scare you," said Deidre. "I wanted to scare you so badly you'd quit the club. I thought if you quit, then I'd get in."

Jenna was furious. "I really trusted you. I can't believe how stupid I've been!"

"I'm so, so sorry," said Deidre. "I know I was

wrong." She held out her hand. "Do you think, maybe, you can forgive me?"

Jenna felt as if someone had knocked the wind out of her. "I don't know," she said. "I thought you were my friend."

"I *was* your friend," said Deidre. "I *am* your friend. I guess I just didn't realize it till now." She still looked as if she might cry. "I'm sorry," she said again. "I wish I'd never—"

Her words were cut off by a sudden *thump* against the door. Deidre gave a little shriek.

"What's that?" demanded Del. "We've got our 'ghost' right here."

"It's what I told you," Deidre said, her pale face even whiter. "I came here to scare you again—to make sure that Jenna would be so frightened she'd quit the club. Only in the snow, I ran into—I ran into the real headless ghost. I ran into Jeb Bendigo."

"Right," said Wendy, her voice full of disbelief.

"It's true," Deidre said. "You've got to believe me! He looked just like the stories said—tall, and dressed in black. He was carrying a pickax. He started chasing me through the woods, chasing me with the pickax . . ."

Marissa stood up and began fixing some of the green and red decorations. "Why should we believe anything you tell us now?"

Deidre was quiet.

"What happened after you ran into the so-called ghost?" Jenna asked.

"He chased me to the front of the lodge. When I tried to get in, he raised his pickax, and I fell." Deidre touched the lump on her head. "I bumped my head and don't remember anything after that until you brought me in here."

"That's a great story, Deidre," said Del. "But I think—"

There was another thump from outside and everyone turned to stare at the door.

"Doesn't anyone believe me?" Deidre cried. She looked terrified.

"I believe you saw something that scared you," said Jenna. "But I just don't believe it was the ghost of Jeb Bendigo."

There was another thump, this time at the side of the lodge.

Even though she was terrified of seeing the headless figure again, Jenna was drawn to the window. After rubbing the window clean all she could see were swirling snowflakes. Then a form took shape and moved toward the window, closer and closer, until it was almost pressed up against the glass.

Jenna tried to still her racing heart. She felt as if every moment since the test of courage had been leading up to this. The tall headless figure was pointing a gloved finger at Jenna. *You*, the gesture seemed to say. *I want you.*

Chapter 16

"It's him!" Deidre screamed. "It's the ghost! He followed me here!"

Jenna just stared at the window. Her heart was beating so fast she wondered if the others could hear it. The thing leaned closer to the window, ran its hand down the glass. *Scratch . . . scratch . . . scratch.*

"It's trying to get in!" Tamara cried.

While the club members watched in terror, the headless thing tried to pull the window up.

"It's locked," Marissa whispered.

The thing tried again to open the window, then shook its fist. A moment later it stepped away from the window.

"It's gone," said Wendy with relief. "Whatever it is, it's gone."

"Don't be too sure," said Deidre. "I thought I got

away from it in the woods. But it kept coming and coming."

Then, as if the ghost had overheard her, there was another loud *thump*.

"We're trapped here," said Wendy, her voice panicky. "We're trapped in a cabin with a headless ghost outside."

"What are we going to do?" asked Danny.

"We're safe as long as we stay here," said Marissa. Her voice was shaking, but she sounded sure of herself as she said, "The windows are locked, the door's locked, there's no way it can get in."

"There's no way we can get out, either," Danny pointed out.

Thump. Thump. Thump.

Now the noises were coming from the front of the lodge by the door.

"He's trying to get in," Deidre whispered. "He's trying to break down the door."

Del picked up the fireplace poker and held it up like a club. Some of the other kids picked up logs and coat hangers. Jenna knew it was hopeless, though. *What kind of weapon could do anything against a ghost?*

Thump.

Everyone was staring at the front door. Staring, and hardly breathing.

"Someone from school will be here soon," said Marissa. "They know we're trapped in the snow. Someone will come to rescue us."

Tamara bit her lip. "What if they don't come in time?"

The thumping got louder and louder until the whole lodge seemed to vibrate.

Then there was a different noise. It sounded like wood cracking. Jenna turned to the door, frozen with fear, as the point of a pickax broke through the door's center.

Chapter 17

The members of the Shadow Club started backing away from the point of the pickax that was sticking through the door.

For a long moment there was no other sound, not even the sound of breathing.

Then, as suddenly as it had appeared, the point of the pickax was gone. All that was left was a hole in the door.

Danny let his breath out with a sigh. "It's gone!"

As if in answer, the ax struck again, breaking a second hole in the door.

"No!" Wendy screamed. "No, no, no! Go away, please, go away!"

The pounding became louder. It came from the front, the back, the sides of the lodge. "It's got us surrounded!" Tamara moaned.

Some of the kids were crying now. "I never really believed in the ghost," Marissa kept repeating.

"Neither did I," said Deidre. "Maybe that's why he's after us."

"No," said Jenna. "That's not why. He's not after you. He's after me." She stood up and put on her ski jacket.

"What are you doing?" asked Marissa.

"I'm going to face the ghost," Jenna said, trying to speak calmly.

"You can't," Wendy said. "He almost killed Deidre. What do you think he'll do to you?"

"Don't you see?" Jenna said. "I have to go out there. I was the one who broke into Jeb Bendigo's cabin. I was the one who stole his treasure."

"But what can you do?" cried Tamara. "How can you fight a ghost?"

"I don't want to fight him," Jenna said. "Somehow I have to find him and—and say I'm sorry."

"We won't let you do it," said Del, standing up. "It's too dangerous!"

"It's more dangerous to stay here and do nothing!" said Jenna, zipping up her jacket. She looked around the room at the circle of frightened faces. *I have to do it,* she told herself. *What's happening is my fault, and I'm the only one who can stop it.*

Jenna took a deep breath and started for the door.

"Wait!" said a voice behind her. Jenna turned and saw Deidre scrambling to her feet. "I'll go with you," Deidre offered.

"Why?" said Jenna. "It's me the ghost is after."

"It's partly my fault," Deidre said. "After all, I made you go into the cabin alone. Maybe it'll be easier if the two of us face him together."

Jenna stared at Deidre. She could tell from her face that Deidre was just as scared as she was. Still, Deidre could be right. Maybe it would be better for the two of them to face the ghost together. "Okay," she said, forcing herself to smile. "Thanks."

Deidre zipped her parka back up and pulled on her boots.

"I don't believe you're doing this," Wendy wailed.

I don't believe it either, thought Jenna. *But it doesn't feel as if I've got much choice*. She looked at Deidre, then walked to the front door and unlocked it. "Ready?"

"As ready as I'll ever be," said Deidre.

Jenna took a deep breath and pulled open the door. A thick gust of snow was blown into the room. Leaving the warm lodge behind, the two girls ran out into the cold, swirling whiteness to meet the ghost.

Chapter 18

The wet snow was so thick that Jenna could hardly breathe. She felt the snow blanket her face. She squinted, trying to see, but all she took in was a wall of white.

"Do you see anything?" Deidre shouted in her ear.

"No!" Jenna shouted back. "Let's check behind the cabin."

Grabbing each other's hands, the girls began to make their way around to the back of the lodge.

As they passed the side window, Jenna looked in at the cheery warmth. For a moment, she wished she were back inside, safe and warm.

Don't even think that way, she told herself. *You have to face the ghost. No one else can do it.*

Jenna and Deidre trudged on through the blizzard.

Jenna kept turning her head, to find any sign of the ghost. All she could see was snow.

They reached the corner of the lodge. There was nothing there. Jenna caught her breath as a dark shape appeared directly in front of them blocking their way.

"No!" Deidre screamed.

Jenna stared, her heart pounding. The dark form swayed to the right, to the left. Then Jenna felt herself relax. "It's just a bush," she told Deidre. "Covered with snow." The bush continued to move, swaying with the wind.

The girls circled around the back side of the lodge. *Where was the ghost? Had it gone back into the woods? Returned to its own cabin?*

"Look!" Deidre suddenly shouted.

Jenna turned to see where Deidre was pointing. Between them and a line of trees stood a tall, dark figure. It was coming toward them, closer and closer.

As the thing drew nearer, Jenna saw that it had no head. It raised its arm, and in its hand was a pickax.

Jenna's heart was pounding so hard she felt her whole body shake. Her knees felt as if they were going to give out. She forced herself not to move as the thing came closer.

It seemed to be in no hurry. It seemed to know there was no way the girls could get away, nowhere they could run.

For a moment Jenna wished she could run back into the lodge, tell everyone the problem was solved, and just sit by the fire, forgetting all about the ghost. But she knew she couldn't. If she didn't settle this, Jeb Bendigo would never leave them alone.

Deidre squeezed her gloved hand, hard. *I'm glad she's here*, Jenna thought.

The ghost moved toward her, its ax held high. Now it was only a few feet away. The wind picked up and the snow swirled even more wildly.

Jenna felt thick flakes stick to her eyelashes as a wave of pure terror went through her. Where the ghost's head should have been, there was nothing. The pickax glittered against the snow.

Here goes, Jenna thought. Her mouth was dry. She had to swallow several times before she could talk. "Jeb Bendigo?" she shouted at the thing.

It didn't answer, but it stopped moving toward her.

"I know why you're here," Jenna went on, using all her courage. "It's because I broke into your cabin. I stole your treasure. I—I just want you to know, I'm sorry. I should never have done it. I'll never do it again. And I'll—I'll return the treasure to you."

The thing stood there, not moving.

"I'll do all those things," Jenna went on, "but please leave me and my friends alone. We're sorry. We're all sorry. None of us knew you were real."

"It's listening," Deidre whispered, squeezing Jenna's hand again.

The headless thing continued to stand as if it were thinking over what Jenna had said. *It listened to me*, she thought. *It understands that I'm sorry. Now, maybe it will go away and—*

"AARGH!" The ghost made a sort of roaring noise, and raised its pickax higher.

"Run!" Jenna shrieked, turning. "Run!"

Deidre turned, too, and the girls stumbled away from the lodge, toward the woods. The snow was so deep it was even hard to walk. Jenna felt as if she were caught in a nightmare, where she could only move in slow-motion.

"Jenna!" Deidre screamed. "It's right behind you!"

Jenna glanced behind her and her throat tightened in fear at what she saw. The thing was almost on top of her. She tried to move faster, but tripped on something buried in the snow. Behind her, the thing swung the pickax. She shut her eyes in terror, then opened them. The ax was sunk in the snow. It had missed her. She scrambled to her feet and tried to run.

The woods, she thought. *If I can get to the woods, maybe I can get away from it. Or at least hide.*

She saw that the ghost seemed to be having as much trouble moving through the snow as she was. Before she could think what that meant, Deidre screamed again.

"Jenna, look out!"

Jenna ducked just as the pickax came sailing through the air. It flew high over her head, then landed harmlessly in a snowdrift.

I've got to make it into the woods, she thought frantically. *I've got to.* The edge of the pine forest appeared through the blizzard. *I'm almost there*, she thought.

Jenna staggered through the blinding snow, no longer able to see where she was going. She hoped she wasn't running in circles. A second later Jenna bumped into something, and she screamed with all her might.

It was the ghost! And it had caught her.

"No!" she screamed. "No, no, no!" She grabbed at the thing's hands, tried to pull them away. It was holding her tightly, though, squeezing the breath from her.

Jenna squirmed, trying to break free. She twisted violently, knocking both herself and the creature to the ground. She didn't even feel the cold, wet snow pushing into her face, filling her eyes, her ears. She just kept fighting with the creature, fighting for her life.

"Leave her alone!" Jenna saw through the swirling snow that Deidre was trying to pull the ghost off her. It was strong, though, stronger than either of them.

Not knowing what else to do, Jenna began kicking at the ghost as hard as she could. To her surprise, it loosened its grip on her. She kicked again and the thing rolled away from her.

"Come on, Jenna!" Deidre shouted. "Run while you have a chance!"

Jenna scrambled to her feet, then stopped. "Wait a minute," she said. She remembered how the ghost had had trouble moving through the snow. How solid it had seemed when she kicked it. "This ghost seems a little too real," she said. Jenna leaned down and grabbed the thing's collar. She pulled hard, ripping off a row of buttons.

The dark coat came open. The bump where the head-less thing's neck should have been wasn't a bump at all. It was a head, wearing a dark ski mask. The thing tried to roll away, but now Deidre was holding it down. Jenna pulled off the ski mask and stared into a familiar face.

"Rob!"

Chapter 19

"Rob!" Jenna cried again.

Her stepbrother looked up at her, breathing hard. He tried to roll away, but she held on to the long coat.

"What are you doing here?" Jenna demanded.

"Let me go!" he shouted, struggling. He was bigger and stronger, but Jenna was not about to let him get away.

"Come on," she called to Deidre. "Help me."

Deidre grabbed Rob's arm. Together the girls began to pull him back toward the lodge.

"All right, all right," he said. "I'm coming."

Jenna's heart was still beating fast, and she was out of breath when they reached the lodge.

Deidre began banging on the door. "Let us in!" she called. "It's me and Jenna."

After a moment the door opened a crack, then all the

way. Del was standing there, the fireplace poker in his hand.

Jenna was happy to see the warm firelight inside. *It's over*, she thought. *It's finally over.* Pushing Rob ahead of her, she entered the lodge.

"What happened?" cried Wendy.

"Did you see the ghost?" said Marissa.

"What's Rob doing here?" asked Danny.

Everyone was talking at once, and Jenna couldn't hear herself think. Deidre stuck her fingers in her mouth and let out a whistle. Everyone stopped talking.

"Come on," said Marissa. "Come over by the fire, all of you."

Jenna followed her over to the fire and took off her wet parka. Rob was frowning. He hadn't said a word.

"Now tell us what happened," said Wendy, pouring hot chocolate for each of them. "What happened with the ghost?"

"There was no ghost," said Jenna. "It was Rob." She glared at her stepbrother, but Rob was staring at the fire, as if he hadn't heard any of them.

"How could it have been Rob?" Del asked. "We all saw it through the window. It didn't have a head."

"It was Rob," Jenna repeated. "He was wearing a dark ski mask with his coat buttoned up over his head."

"I don't believe this," said Marissa. "Are you saying *two* people have been pretending to be the ghost of Jeb Bendigo?"

James grinned. "Three, if you count my little performance."

Jenna turned to Deidre. "Why didn't you tell us Rob was in on it, too?"

"I didn't know," said Deidre. She seemed to be as confused as the others. "Rob, what's going on?"

"It was because of you," Rob said, finally speaking.

"Me?" said Deidre.

"I saw you, the first night you dressed up as the ghost," he said. "I was coming back from the gym. I'd been shooting hoops in the gym, after hours. I didn't want to get caught, so I was sneaking through the woods. I saw someone standing in front of the building opposite Jenna's window, dressed as the ghost. Then I watched when you went into the woods and took off the disguise."

"Why didn't you tell me?" asked Jenna.

Rob's voice dropped so low, Jenna could barely hear it. "It gave me an idea," he said. "I had asked my dad to let me go home to California. But he said he thought it was best if you and I were in the same school. He thought you would help me do better in school. So I decided if Deidre scared you enough, you would want to leave Phantom Valley."

"But—" Jenna stopped. "So you thought if I asked to leave, our folks would let you go home, too."

"It was worth a try," said Rob. "You know how much I hate it here."

"So you knew all along," Jenna said. "You knew

Deidre was doing all those awful things. And you didn't tell me or try to stop her."

"I didn't actually see her do all of them," Rob said. "But sure I knew. Only Deidre didn't know I knew. I started reading stories about the headless ghost. I didn't want to hurt you or anything. I just wanted to scare you. Only you wouldn't scare."

"I was scared all right," said Jenna. "I just wasn't sure it was a ghost."

"That's why I decided to come out here today," Rob went on. "I figured if I could scare everyone in the club, you'd have to believe a ghost was after you."

"Only you ran into Deidre."

Rob nodded. "Since she wasn't able to make you believe there was a ghost, I decided to scare *her*. I thought that would convince you."

"It almost did," said Jenna.

"Anyway, I just want you to know I'm sorry," Rob said, sad and embarrassed. "It's not your fault I wound up at Chilleen. And it was lousy of me to try to scare you away from a school you really like. I've been a real jerk."

Jenna wasn't sure what to say. Rob and Deidre had made the last few weeks of her life a nightmare. And yet she knew she couldn't stay mad at either of them. It was hard to believe they could both be so unhappy. "Maybe it will help if I talk to our folks," she said to her stepbrother. "I don't want to leave Chilleen, but maybe they will let you go back home." She turned and stared into the fire for a moment.

"This is totally weird," said Wendy after a moment. "I really thought there was a ghost."

"We all did," said Jenna. "Everyone but Deidre and Rob."

"So there's no headless ghost after all," Del said. "It's kind of disappointing."

Danny stood up. "While we're clearing up mysteries," he said, "what was that 'blood' we drank?"

Marissa smiled. "Peach juice with red food-coloring and salt."

Yuck! thought Jenna.

"And Bendigo's head?" Deidre asked.

"A trick I created with a ball, a mask, and glow-in-the-dark paint," Del admitted.

There was a sudden pounding at the door.

For a moment no one moved.

Finally Del opened the door. Mr. Tam, dressed in a heavy parka, stood there, covered in snow.

"I've come to rescue you," he said. "I've got a four-wheel-drive vehicle."

His announcement was greeted with groans and boos. "I wanted to be snowed in the whole weekend," said Tamara.

"Come on," Mr. Tam said. "Let's put the fire out and gather up your things. The storm's getting worse."

The others grumbled, but began packing. Jenna's parka was still wet, but she slipped it back on. She didn't say anything, but she was glad Mr. Tam had come. She'd had enough of the Shadow Club. Somehow, the club had stopped mattering to her.

"Bye, Rob." Jenna smiled at her stepbrother as the taxi from Silverbell pulled up to take him to the airport.

Rob grinned at her. "Sure you don't want to come with me?"

"Very sure," Jenna answered. She and Jeff picked up Rob's carry-on bags and followed him to the end of the drive. "Remember, I like it here," she said, grinning.

"Even without the Shadow Club?" Rob teased.

"Definitely without the Shadow Club!"

"I still can't believe you quit," Jeff said.

Jenna shrugged. "It was mostly pranks and gossip. It wasn't all that great once I got in."

"I heard they decided not to pick anyone as a replacement for you," Jeff said. "They'll wait till next semester before choosing new members."

"That must have upset Deidre," Rob said.

"I don't think so," said Jenna. "Deidre isn't too thrilled with them, either. She even told her father they're just a bunch of snobs."

"Told you," Rob said.

Rob and Jeff helped the driver load the bags into the trunk, then Rob turned to Jenna. "Thanks again for talking to the folks. They listened to you."

"No problem," Jenna said. "I'm glad you're going to be where you want to be."

"Me, too. I can't believe I'm saying this, but I think I'm going to miss you."

"I'll see you during summer break," Jenna told him. "And just in case you decide you miss Chilleen, I promise the first thing I'll do when I get home is make you a big pot of soup!"

About the Author

LYNN BEACH was born in El Paso, Texas, and grew up in Tucson, Arizona. She is the author of many fiction and nonfiction books for adults and children.